I0615483

Eliza Allen Starr

Christmas-Tide

Eliza Allen Starr

Christmas-Tide

ISBN/EAN: 9783743419544

Manufactured in Europe, USA, Canada, Australia, Japa

Cover: Foto ©Andreas Hilbeck / pixelio.de

Manufactured and distributed by brebook publishing software
(www.brebook.com)

Eliza Allen Starr

Christmas-Tide

CHRISTMAS - TIDE.

BY

ELIZA ALLEN STARR,

Author of "Patron Saints," "Pilgrims and Shrines," "Songs of
a Life Time," "Isabella of Castile," "Christian
Art in Our Own Age."

PUBLISHED BY THE AUTHOR.
SAINT JOSEPH'S COTTAGE NO. 299 HURON STREET,
CHICAGO, ILLINOIS,
1891.

TO THE MEMORY

OF THAT

DAUNTLESS CHRISTIAN KNIGHT

AND

LEAL CHAMPION OF OUR LADY,

JAMES McMASTER.

These pages, written under his chivalrous patronage,
are dedicated, with a
Requiescat in pace

BY THE AUTHOR.

SAINT JOSEPH'S COTTAGE,
FEAST OF OUR LADY OF MOUNT CARMEL,
1891.

CONTENTS.

ILLUSTRATION.

(ON COVER.)

AFTER LUCA DELLA ROBBIA.

CHRISTMAS.

I.

Merrie Christmas! Christmas with its carols, its chimes, its evergreen garlands, its laurel and holly and its mistletoe bough! Christmas with its Yule-log, its Santa Claus, its charming surprises, its lovely gifts! Christmas with its family gatherings, its tall tree of spruce or pine or hemlock for the little folk! Christmas with its snow-banks and icicles and glorious sunshine! This is the American Christmas; the Christmas which has become universal in our land, from Maine to Louisiana, Texas, California; from the Atlantic to the Pacific. The Christmas of the descendants of those who came over in the Mayflower, in the December of 1620,

Reprinted from THE FREEMAN'S JOURNAL by the courtesy of the present Editors, the Messrs. Ford.

as well as of those who landed in Jamestown, in 1607. In staid villages where, thirty years ago, the December Christmas was not thought of beside the Thanksgiving Day of November, and where, still less, was there ever a garland of evergreen woven in its honor, Christmas cards are now one of the necessities of the season, and "Merrie Christmas!" flies from neighbor to neighbor, as if the heart could never weary of the joyous greeting. And yet, is this American Christmas quite after the ideal which has given to the world that *Venite Adoremus* which thrills us every Christmas morning as if we heard it for the first time, calling us to hasten with the shepherds to Bethlehem, to the Crib? That ideal Christmas which inspired Correggio's *Notte*, that night of nights, with its midnight shadows, its Babe radiating celestial splendors, its ecstatic Virgin Mother; a *Venite Adoremus* perpetuated to the eye? And not only Correggio's; but, long, long before him, those Nativities in the illuminated missals and antiphonals of the monastic centres of art which gave types to a Niccolo Pisano, a Cimabue, a Giotto, an Andrea Pisano, a Luca della Robbia, a Lorenzo di Credi, a Perugino, a Raphael; while the types of these very cloisters ran back to mysterious sources hidden for hundreds of years, but now laid open to view on the torchlit walls of some catacomb of the Apostolic age, like that of Saint Priscilla or of Saint Domitilla. Looking back over the art, still more, the Liturgy of these almost nineteen hundred years, do we not feel that the popular Christmas of America lacks some essential element which gave this festival a hold on the imaginations and consciences of Christians; and that, while our Christmas is merry and kindly, and poetic too, if you will, it is not, in the popular mind, a religious festival?

The Catholic American of to-day is like a voyager among the beautiful coral reefs; he must often drop his sounding-line. The tide of immigration brings thousands of Catholics to our shores; but, either they leave their traditions of fasts and feasts behind them, or forget them on coming among new scenes; and there is not one festival or solemnity of their religion which would not fail of its essential characteristic as to circumstances, but for that Liturgy, which is like the pilot at the helm, not only of the Church, but of Christian society. The sorrow and the mortification is, that so few Catholics take the trouble to understand this Liturgy, or to enter into its spirit. For most people, it is enough that the ceremonies of the Church go on, and that they attend upon those of obligation; but as to any curiosity concerning the meaning of these ceremonies, it seems hardly to exist. Only when an unusual representation or

symbol is presented, some memory is revived
of the beautiful old Catholic countries from
which they have come, in pursuit of wealth or of
competency, to find themselves stripped of
everything pertaining to their glorious old
Faith but its creed. To-day, every intelligent
Catholic has a work to do; which is, to connect
himself and his family with the traditions of the
Church, so that her festivals will be kept, not
according to provincial or even national customs, but according to that grand ceremonial
which has set a crown of beauty on the civilization of the past ages of the Church, and is to do
so for the future, even in the United States of
America. "Happy," says M. Rio, in one of
the chapters of his *L'Art Chretien*, "happy is
the people whose national and religious traditions are identical." Happy indeed; but
those who are not thus favored have but one
course to pursue—to engraft on a noble, natural
stock the still more august traditions of an ancient Faith.

To learn, then, the true spirit of the Christian
festivals we must turn to the Liturgy itself; a Liturgy which, as Dom Guéranger states so concisely,
is " drawn from three sources, the Old and New
Testaments, and that new song which the Church
remembering that to her, also, has been given
the trumpet and the harp," so devoutly sings
through her doctors and such inspired poets as

Prudentius and Thomas Aquinas. As one sees
at a glance, this Liturgy, which is like the shell
to the essential Faith and essential Sacraments
given by Our Lord Himself through His Apostles, and which dates its *Dominus Vobiscum*
and *Orate, fratres,* to Pope Clement, martyred
in the year A. D. 100; and has been ever since,
enriched by new offices for new feasts and new
saints, is the repository of the Christian traditions from the Apostolic times to our own. To
this we can turn to know what spirit we should
be of at every ecclesiastical season; and to
know the Liturgy of the Church, is to know
what is worth knowing in all the prayer-books
in the world. It is, in fact, the one prayer-book
which every educated Catholic should possess;
and it is the one which even the unlettered, in
Catholic countries, know by hearing and seeing.
It is, then, to this Liturgy that we must look to
learn the true spirit of Christmas; and first, we
will speak of those four weeks of preparation,
typical of the four thousand years before the
birth of Our Lord, known as Advent. We find
that this season of Advent, so early as the
fifth century, was really a season of penance.
Special sermons were preached, fasting prac-
ticed three times a week from Martinmas, November 11th, until Christmas. In the twelfth
century this fast was reduced to an abstinence;
and, finally, both fast and abstinence have been

removed from the weak shoulders of modern Christians. But while this lessening of penitential practices has been going on in reference to the laity, the Church preserves, intact, the spirit of her Liturgy. The vestments for Advent are purple, the very same as in Lent; the *Gloria in excelsis Deo* is no longer heard; at the end of Mass, instead of the *Ita missa est*, the people are dismissed with the *Benedicamus Domino;* the *Alleluia* is still retained; but in churches where the music is rubrical, the organ is not heard excepting on the third Sunday of Advent, when rose-colored vestments are allowed. But to compensate for these losses, nothing could be more beautiful than the Introits and Antiphons of Advent. The *Rorate,* " Drop down dew, ye heavens, and let the clouds rain the just; let the earth be opened and bud forth a Saviour," seizes the imagination as if it had but now fallen from the inspired lips of Isaiah. In the French churches is sung a wonderfully beautiful chant founded upon this Introit, which we have listened to, Advent after Advent, in monastic churches in America; a chant which lives in the memory by reason of its plaintive chords, full of supplication, even when the full beauty of its phrases is not known as when read. With the Introits comes a tender refrain from the Psalms: *Qui regis intende;* " Give ear, O Thou that rulest Israel; Thou that

leadest Joseph like a sheep;" and still another :
Veni et ostende: Come, O Lord, show us Thy
face;" the very sigh which we can imagine
must have come from the heart of the Virgin
Mother on the feast of her Expectation, when
the *Rorate* again makes the Introit. In the
Vesperal Antiphons, however, breathes a spirit
so sublime that they may be said to unite in
themselves the most exalted sentences from the
Prophecies and Psalms; especially the Seven
Greater Antiphons, or the " O's of Advent," as
they are sometimes called, because all the seven
begin with this same ejaculation, sung at the
Magnificat or Canticle of the Blessed Virgin,
from December 17th to 23d, inclusive. We give
them entire as too precious to be withheld :

" O Wisdom, that comest out of the mouth of
the Most High, that reachest from one end to
another, and dost mightily and sweetly order all
things: come and teach us the way of prudence !

"O Adonai, and Ruler of the house of Israel,
who didst appear unto Moses in the burning
bush, and gavest him the law in Sinai: come
to redeem us with an outstretched arm !

" O Root of Jesse, which standest for an en-
sign of the people, at whom the kings shall shut
their mouths, and unto whom the Gentiles shall
seek: come to deliver us, make no tarrying.

" O Key of David, and Sceptre of the house of
Israel; that openest and no man shutteth; and

shuttest and no man openeth: come, to bring out the prisoners from prison, and them that sit in darkness, and in the shadow of death.

"O Day-spring, brightness of the everlasting light, Sun of Righteousness: come, to give light to them that sit in darkness and the shadow of death!

"O King of the Gentiles, yea and desire thereof, O Corner-stone that makest of two one: come to save man, whom Thou hast made of the dust of the earth!"

"O Emmanuel, our King and our Law-giver, longing of the Gentiles, yea and salvation thereof: come to save us, O Lord our God!"

All the prophetic grandeur of the Old Testament, from Genesis to the Maccabees, and all the joy of fulfillment in the New, are gathered, pressed, into these Antiphons—these anthems as they might be called; and give us an idea of the sublimity which runs through the whole divine office; a school, in itself, of everything which can ennoble the soul and heart, and which may well make of the priest who feeds daily on this honey of wisdom, an angel in mind and in manners.

These Antiphons bring us to the Vigil of Christmas—that Christmas Eve which is a signal for merriment and festivity throughout the land. The shops are so many *parterres*, as to color and variety, all the day long; and twilight brings a blaze of light over these wonders of the loom and the handicraft of the nations; for there is not one on the face of the earth which does not give its skill to the shops of Christmas Eve. Formerly the stockings,

"Hung round the chimney with care,"

were the authorized mediums for the Christmas gifts, waiting for the morning to reveal their treasures. But of late the Eve itself is the time when Christmas-trees are all a-light, and every child's eyes open to catch the first gleam of tiny red and blue candles, and the prettiness of all sorts that sparkles and twinkles in too many forms to be described, from the boughs of this wonderful tree! The home festivities have begun with cakes and sugars, while on the streets of our great cities, midnight finds buyers and sellers still busy. This is the popular Christmas Eve of to-day. Does it seem too joyous to disturb? If the ear has taken in all the solemnity of the Greater Antiphons, if the soul has come within the tender twilight of the four weeks of Advent, if the *Rorate* has touched the germ of a living expectation, there will be something in all this which jars upon a certain sensibility developed in the mind, in the heart. For, during the last three days where have we been in imagination? With that tender Virgin Mother and her spouse, Saint Joseph, who have left the Holy House of Nazareth to answer to

the summons of the Roman Cæsar, calling upon
all the world to come, each to his own city, to
be enrolled, that Cæsar may know over how
many he rules. Gently, indeed, does the soft-
paced mule bear the double burden of Mary
and her unborn Babe. Reverently, too, does
Joseph walk at her side, meditating on the wonderful mystery transpiring under his protection.
But the weary way does not shorten, nor do the
hardships of the season lessen as they go on.
He who made the frost and cold and stormy
winds for His own praise, abates nothing of
their force when turned against Himself, and,
with those nearest Him, is their victim. The
journey which may have seemed short to Joseph
many a time before, has seemed, now, well
nigh interminable. But it is coming to an end.
Already, as the short day retires and the swift-
footed night approaches, the lights gleam out
from Bethlehem—David's city, the city of Mary
and Joseph as descendants of this same king
of Judah; and the name of this city means none
other than the "House of Bread;" as if hos-
pitality were its characteristic. The patient
mule steps more lightly along the frosty path;
there is a promise of rest for the beast and for
his double burden. Already the eyes of Saint
Joseph have fastened on the spot where he ex-
pects to find an open door and a welcome, and
an evening meal ready to be served; and thus

he enters the narrow streets of Bethlehem of
Judah, out of which is "to come the Ruler."
How the first refusal must have fallen on his
heart like lead! Then another and another,
until, withered by the unkindness of his countrymen and even kinsmen, not towards himself,
but his precious charge, he looks into the face
of Mary, the Virgin of fifteen, to be re-assured,
transported! Whence is that light which glows
all over her beautiful young face? Whence
that serenity which sits enthroned on her brow?
that ecstacy of contentment in her virginal
eyes? Enough. The heart of Joseph is again
strong. He no longer knocks at inhospitable
doors to be refused; but, with a meekness
sweeter than that of Moses when he bore with
the children of Israel, he turns through the
winding streets of the town to a sheltered cave
on its lonely edge, where the ox and the ass have
been left by their owner for the wintry night.
What man had refused, the dumb beasts allow
them to share; and it is here, in the rude stable and beside the manger, that the Church and
her children put themselves in spirit on Christmas Eve. It is in memory of the inhospitality
of Bethlehem and the hardships of that day's
journey and of the cave, that the Church keeps
her vigil and her fast; a fast exceeded in
strictness only by that of Good Friday. It is to
the un-illumined cave that she calls the Chris-

tian world, its fathers and mothers, sons, daughters, and little ones, of all degrees; and in all the Catholic cities of Europe what do we see on Christmas Eve? In Paris itself—gay, worldly Paris, which is called infidel—the crowds turn, as midnight approaches, not to the wonted marts of toys and trifles, of elegancies and luxuries, but towards Notre Dame, Saint Roche, the Madeleine, Saint Germain, towards all her great churches. On that night, the most timid can walk in safety along her boulevards, or her narrowest streets, for one mind seems to possess the crowd; while in Rome, who can give an idea of the living streams which set, more than all, towards Saint Mary Major, on the Esquiline Hill? Not the first Saint Mary's of Rome; that belongs to the Trastevere; but the largest of eighty churches within her limits which bear that beloved name, or Saint Mary's of the Crib, as it is also called; for there Rome venerates the Crib discovered by Saint Helen.

No one can fail to see, by all this, how utterly the idea of a social festival, a family gathering, is lost in the abyss of the mystery in which the festival begins; an abyss into which myriads of angels looked only to fall, while others beheld it for their everlasting reward; for it is the mystery of the Incarnation! Just so far as the Incarnation is a well-spring of Christian thought and practice, just so far is the

Christmas festival a religious rather than a domestic one. It is only when the idea of the household dominates over that of the Christian family, that Christmas loses its distinctive type, and is merged into the list of merry-makings. Of the awful degradation effected in the mind of a community, of a nation, by such an exchange, it is impossible to speak worthily. It is to drag down to a merely natural plane the most sublime and the most significant of supernatural facts. It is to uncrown the noblest idealities of the human race. It is to ignore the only tradition which can keep alive the understanding of the supernatural creation and the supernatural redemption of the human race. In this country, only within the precincts of a convent have we ever seen a Christmas Eve according to our ideal, according to what poets have sung and inspired artists have painted. This ideal is preserved in the world but too seldom, we fear, excepting in places remote from towns. We know of one spot where a chapel stands close to what might be called a chateau, with its high, overhanging roof, its piazzas, its domain of wood and field, of hill and valley, of running brook and far off lakeshore, where the break of the waves may be heard at midday. And in this chapel, where many a mass has been said on week-days and lesser festivals, the Christmas vigil is kept as strictly as in a convent. Here, the altar-piece is a Nativity, and the Christmas garlands and decorations make a cave for the Virgin Mother; and here, until the stroke of midnight, all is silence, darkness and meditation. Then all is light and joy and praise! But we must tell of one other holy solitude, where years ago, one who is both a poet and an artist settled with his family, in a home built, literally by their own hands. When Christmas was near, a surprise was prepared for the little ones; but how different from the toy-laden tree which keeps so many little folk awake in anticipation!

There were no stockings, even, hung around the huge chimney, but the young ones were taken from their low beds, wrapped in blankets and set before a mysterious screen. Just at midnight the screen vanished and before them was an almost breathing picture of that Babe who had chosen, almost nineteen centuries ago, to be born in a stable and to be cradled in a manger! It was as if a vision met their eyes, so blinded were they by the sudden brightness, and an "Oh!" of awe and of rapture broke from their lips as they shaded their eyes to look still more intently at the vision. In both of these lovely solitudes the tradition of Christmas has been kept; and no one can say that the Christmas had lost anything at their hands of poetry, of impressiveness or of delight. Nor could such Christmases ever be forgotten or ever merge themselves in the festive recollections of other festive seasons. Forever and forever, that Christmas altar in the home chapel, that picture of the Divine Infant on His bed of straw, on the walls of the secluded Wisconsin homestead, will live in the memories of the children of those households; and the experiences of life in other lands or communities, rich in art, and in all the circumstances which foster the ideal, will only deepen the impression, and thus make one the associations of childhood and those of the pilgrim to the noblest shrines of Christendom. There will be no missing link in the religious traditions of such a life, beginning with the Incarnation. The immeasurable dignity and fruitfulness of such traditions above those which are now so popular among us, is one on which we may well allow our thoughts to dwell, until Bethlehem is incorporated into the innermost tissue of our everyday life.

Some one has said that the charm of the sunrise is over when the sun has risen. But what shall we say of that Midnight Mass which is like the glory of a newly-risen sun? How well we remember our hurried steps over the crispy snow of December on our way to the near city convent a little before midnight! or the gliding with veiled nuns along the galleries of a convent far from towns, in a silence known only among religious, to the chapel which was itself a cave, but which was suddenly illuminated as the bell struck for midnight, all the altars blazing with candles! How the *Venite Adoremus* was more than sweet music! how the garlands and the flowers and the incense were more than decorations! the expressions of a joy too deep for words, and which welled over in tears! And we remember, too a Midnight Mass within twenty-four hours of our landing on shore, after six tempest-tost weeks on the ocean—when thousands within the sacred fane were hushed as one tranced being, and when the songs of angels seemed the only music. The Child was born; the midnight of the Cave had disappeared; we were among the shepherds, with Mary and Joseph beside the Crib! It was the fulfillment of an ocean Advent of expectation; and the joy of Christmas was there, although not one in that strange land might have for us a "Merrie Christmas!"

One of the most touching customs for Christmas is that of preparing a Crib in some part of the church; which dates to that seraphic lover of holy poverty, Saint Francis of Assisi. We are told that, stirred as he was in his own soul by the tenderest sympathy for the little Infant shivering in the.Cave of Bethlehem in the December midnight, he caught the idea of making all this present and real to the eyes of his disciples. A cave was prepared; a manger was filled with straw; the ox and the ass took their places beside it. On the straw lay the radiant Child so lowly in His majesty, and beside Him His Virgin Mother and her virgin spouse and the simple shepherds. How poor it all was—must have been—from all we know of Saint Francis and of what he was likely to do! "How inadequate!" no doubt some of those said whose ingenuity had been taxed to prepare it. But when midnight came and the Midnight Mass, and when Saint Francis rose to preach to them with the Crib in sight, who can ever tell the wonderful effect of that Christmas sermon! Transported out of himself, he took all his listeners with him, and the whole churchful of religious prostrated themselves before the Infant in his Manger-Crib. From the convent of Saint Francis the custom spread all over Christendom. Churches, monasteries, convents, homes, castles and cabins, had each its representation of the Crib. It was the stable, the manger, the meekness of Saint Joseph, the rapture of the Virgin Mother, the absolute poverty of the Holy Family, which Saint Francis put before his followers. And we must do as Saint Francis did, if we would win souls to the simplicity of the Cave and the Holy Infancy. It can never be too humble to draw the hearts of the multitude, who press around it with a rapture of love and reparation which no grand painting or representation of any other sort could ever inspire.

In the United States, the Midnight Mass is said in churches at 4 or 5 o'clock in the morning, and is followed immediately by the "Mass of the Aurora," as it is called. In ancient times, the Pope went directly from his Midnight Mass to the Church of Saint Anastasia, who was martyred on the 25th of December, 303, and the second Collect of this Mass still keeps her in distinguished remembrance. The third or Solemn High Mass has so many graces attached to it, that we can not allow even the weariness which comes after the early Masses to prevail against us. Every priest has the privilege of saying three Masses on Christmas Day; and it should be considered the privilege of every Christian to assist at three Masses, if possible. Nor can any one be indifferent to the significance, as well as the beauty and the grandeur, of this Mass, for is it not the triumphal song of the Incarnation? That Incarnation, which began in the obscurity and silence of a room in the Holy House of Nazareth, was fulfilled in the gloom and the humiliation of a stable, but is now glorified to the eyes of all men by the magnificence of altars, of golden vestments, and if in a cathedral by all the solemnity of Pontifical ceremonial. If we have entered the stable to adore the Divine Infant in the Crib, it will relieve the wish of the heart to do something in honor of this little Babe, this

Incarnate Word, who "came unto His own, and His own receieved Him not," to assist at the Grand Third Mass of Christmas. We shall, instinctively, offer it in expiation for that ignorance which shut against Him the doors of the pleasant homes of Bethlehem, that ignorance which leaves Him, even now unrecognized by so many kindly hearts in the world which is called Christian; which cuts short His claims to worship and obedience, and even while Christmas greetings are sounding in our ears, makes Him forgotten in the love of worldly enjoyments. It will be just one little act of reparation to the Babe in the manger; and how precious is every such act, however small. Years ago, a little girl, scarcely four years old was in the habit of stealing to our side as we said our prayers. One day she asked about a picture of the Nativity which hung near. In as simple words as we could, we told her about the Babe born in a stable because no one had any room in their houses for His Mother; and how, when He grew up, He was put to death by cruel men, all because of His goodness. This child had never been baptized and "must not be proselyted;" but no sooner did this natural story come to her ears than her eyes filled with tears, and throwing up her childish arms she cried out: "Let me kiss the little Jesus baby again!" It was the true spirit of reparation;

and that kiss, we believe, has never been, never will be, forgotten by Him who lay in His Crib in the Stable of Bethlehem. This spirit of reparation, which is so simple, and so natural, that a child practices it instinctively, inspires the sweetest and the most sublime offerings made by man to God; and while the most hidden, they are the most powerful to win graces for ourselves or for others. This was the offering of His Virgin Mother, of His foster father, who endeavored to supply the lack of love in others by the fervor of their own ; and this is our offering when we attend the Solemn High Mass, or better still, the Pontifical Mass, in honor of the " Word made flesh and dwelling among us." As a reward for all this, instant and full, comes the Papal Benediction, bestowed on Christmas Day upon all who, having con- fessed and communicated, have paid the hom- age of adoration to the Infant Jesus.

But what of that even-song, the magnificent "Second Vespers" of Christmas? Is it possible that our dinners on that day are so elaborate as to give us no time to assist at Vespers? Is it possible that we have so many and such dig- nified guests—guests so indifferent themselves to the Liturgy of the day—that we can not join in the Blessed Virgin's own *Magnificat*, and that the Antiphons of this great day are to be lost for us? Is it possible that anything which the world calls pleasure can keep us from that Manger-Crib where lies the Infant who is to redeem us and all we hold dear? Has He lost His charm so soon? Is there nothing in that smile which draws us irresistibly from the luxurious home and makes us almost weep to think how comfortable it is; still more from the groaning tables of the banquet? Let us steal away from all these for awhile, and see how the Church attires herself, with her Pontiffs, to sing the praises of her Infant King.

Those who recited the dramatic Third Responsory at Matins:

"O ye shepherds, speak, and tell us what ye have seen; who is appeared in the earth?

We saw the new-born Child, and Angels singing praise to the Lord.

Speak; what have ye seen? And tell us of the Birth of Christ.

We saw the new-born Child, and Angels singing praise to the Lord.

Glory be to the Father, and to the Son, and to the Holy Ghost.

We saw the new-born Child, and Angels singing praise to the Lord,"—will enter into the spirit of the Antiphons at Vespers.

"*First Antiphon.*—Thine shall be the dominion in the day of Thy power, amid the brightness of the saints; from the womb, before the day-star, have I begotten Thee.

Second Antiphon.—The Lord sent redemption unto His people, He hath commanded His covenant forever.

Third Antiphon.—Unto the upright hath arisen light in darkness; the Lord is gracious, and full of compassion, and righteous.

Fourth Antiphon.—With the Lord there is mercy, and with Him is plenteous redemption.

Fifth Antiphon.—Of the fruit of Thy body will I set upon Thy throne.

Antiphon at the Song of the Blessed Virgin.— This day the Christ is born: this day the Saviour is appeared: this day the Angels sing praise in the earth, and the Archangels rejoice: this day the righteous are glad and say: Glory to God in the highest. Alleluia.''

And each one set to its own celestial music, sung ages ago, as to-day, by choirs loving the chaste melodies they sang! No one can rightfully forego these sacred chants for any worldly reason; for the feast was given for this very end—the praise of the Babe of Bethlehem. To claim the feast, yet to neglect its intention, is one of the—shall we say sins, or blunders, of our time?

When we give ourselves time to study the Divine Office, we find it a composition so wonderful in its parts, with such a decorum in the carrying out of its festivals, that we are reminded of the dignified action of the Greek drama. One of the most striking examples of this is that of rounding out a festival by an *Octave*. The eighth day brings back enough of the glory of the feast not only to revive devotion, but to secure its fruits; while every day of the Octave is a sweet and gentle reminder of it. The Octave of Christmas does not confine itself to the repetition of the festival, but gives, first: the Feast of Saint Stephen, the first martyr, whose relics lie in Rome under the High Altar in the center of the largest rotunda of the world. All around this proto-martyr, on the vast walls bare of other ornament, are representations of the martyrdoms of the three first Christian centuries; and here the Romans bring their children to teach them how to die for their Faith, while on the walls of the little "Golden Chapel" of Nicholas V., in the Vatican, Fra Angelico left his tribute of honor to the first martyr in one of the most perfect frescoes which ever came from his hand. The second feast is that of Saint John, Apostle and Evangelist, and the third is that of the "Holy Innocents," the "*Childermas*" of our ancestors. In our times, the popular mind is too sensitive to allow it to dwell upon the pathetic details of this event, and no artist thinks of reproducing it. But in the ages of the revival this was a favorite subject, and taken literally from Saint Matthew. It is to be seen on the floor of the

Cathedral at Siena, represented with wonderful
delicacy as to execution, and is, at the same
time, most powerful in action. Unlike many,
even of the Florentine school, it is, indeed, hor-
rible as to cruelty, but without grossness; and
the mothers vainly endeavor to protect their
children, not as lionesses, but as broken-hearted,
distracted mothers. On the inner wall of that
same Saint Stephen of the Rotunda on the
Cœlian Hill, where lie the relics of the first
martyr, we find the Holy Innocents. The first
picture as we turn from the small side altar of
SS. Primus and Feliciamus, where are exquisite
mosaics representing these saints, is that of the
Crucifixion; and at the feet of our Lord, the
King of martyrs, lie the Holy Innocents who
suffered for Him. Fra Angelico, with all his gentleness of soul, treated this subject in one of
the choral books of his monastery as an actual
event going on under the eyes; but in one of
the choral books of the ancient Church of
Saint Ambrose at Milan it is a remembered
event, and the Holy Innocents are seen with
palms in their hands, and the blood trickling
from their throats, while they sing their song of
deliverance "from the snare of the fowler."
But far back of these pictures as to date, is the
old mosaic of the Holy Innocents in the Church
of Saint Paul Outside the Walls; while it is one
of the events, closely connected with the Incar-

nation, represented among the mosaics of the triumphal arch of Saint Mary Major, erected in the fifth century under Sixtus III. The beautiful asylum for orphans on the *Piazza Annunziata*, Florence, called the Hospital of the Holy Innocents, has for an altar-piece one of the two pictures painted by Ghirlandajo representing the Holy Innocents; and on each of the spandrels between the arches of the arcade which makes the beauty of its front is represented, in terra-cotta relief by Andrea della Robbia, an Innocent in swaddling clothes. And yet all these tributes of the pictorial art are antedated by the Hymn of Prudentius, the poet of the fourth century, which still makes one of the Breviary hymns, and certain verses of which, beginning with:

"Lovely flowers of martyrs, hail!"

every child should learn before leaving the nursery. But the Romans of to-day are not satisfied to leave the story of the Holy Innocents to past ages. The day of their feast is honored in a way to give children the precedence in the public eye. On this day the little Roman acolyte believes himself the "observed of all observers;" for on this day the Roman boys preach sermons, after the manner of great orators, in the ancient Church of Ara Cœli, close by the Capitol. The special fitness of this church is evident, so soon as we remember that one of its altars stands where, according to the old Roman tradition, stood one raised by Augustus to the mysterious Being who would be born of a Virgin, as declared by the sibyl whom he had consulted; and to the Franciscans, who took from their holy founder such a special devotion to the Holy Infancy and the Crib, belongs, very properly, in their office as guardians of the *Ara Cœli* and the *Bambino*, or Infant, the keeping up of this commemoration of the Holy Innocents among the Roman boys.

Of the Octave of Christmas, the Feast of the Circumcision, it is almost useless to speak at present. The Christian tradition is so completely absorbed in the social, that it comes to most Catholics, even, especially when observed only as a day of devotion, as the beginning of the New Year, with all the festivities of open house and open doors; a custom gracious and innocent, when not carried to excess. Our Lord in His Crib was very patient with men. He exacted very little. This may be a motive for some tender spirit to give more than is exacted; and there is no one who should not honor the mystery of the first blood-shedding of Our Lord by assisting at the Holy Sacrifice on that day, even in dioceses where it is not of obligation.

II.

It is the vigil of Christmas, and we are in Rome! The Advent fast and abstinence has not yet been broken; even the children have not had their boxes of *bon bons*, and the joy of anticipation which pervades all hearts, has a certain tender solemnity in it which chastens the smile and throws a hush over the household. The slender evening collation has been taken, and we hasten—where? To what church of the Eternal City shall we hasten to-night —not for the Midnight Mass, which is not permitted in the churches, but for that Mass which precedes midnight, and leaves us at that hour in an ecstasy before the "Child born to us, a Saviour?" Where, we repeat, but to the church of all churches, which keeps the

35

memory of the Incarnation and Nativity before
the eyes of the Christian world, and has done so
from its foundation—*Sancta Maria ad Nives*,
or "Saint Mary of the Snow;"* *Santa Maria
Maggiore*, "Saint Mary Major" or "The Great
Saint Mary's;" and known by another, and to-
night still dearer name, *Sancta Maria ad Praesepe*, or "Saint Mary of the Crib?" For here is
treasured the rough manger in which Mary,
Virgin Mother, cradled her Divine Son when she
had wrapped Him in His swaddling-clothes. It
is then to *Sancta Maria Praesepe* that we turn
our steps to-night, and oh, how near we seem to
come, in Rome, to Bethlehem and its Stable!
We pause a momont on the summit of the
Quattro Fontane, and look down on the grand
old Basilica, founded in the year 352, and ever
since the delight of Christendom ; and as we look
down and see, dimly defined, the tall campanile,
the twin domes, the outline of the vast church,
and even the obelisk of ancient Egypt, we feel
as if we belonged to the band of shepherds that
watched their flocks by night and heard the first
Gloria in excelsis Deo, then looked toward Bethlehem, as told by the angel, to see a lambent

---

* So called because its site and area were determined by a
miraculous fall of snow on the 5th of August, 351. All this
was indicated by a vision or dream sent on that same night to
Patrician John and his wife and Pope Liberius. Ancient
mosaics on the exterior wall of the basilica represent the three
dreams, as identically the same, and also the founding of the
church.

light above the town : for in the darkness of the
late hour the lights from within give forth a
luminous atmosphere, like that which fills and
even surrounds the Stable of Bethlehem in the
pictures of the great Christian masters.

The pause is only for a moment, and we take,
instinctively, the swift pace of the crowds hurry-
ing in the same direction and for the same pur-
pose. But as we walk quickly past the obelisk,
too swiftly to turn our eyes even, the inscriptions
come back to us with a meaning never realized
before.* On entering the church, it seems to
have been transformed ; still more, all its decorations stand forth with a significance we have
passed over in the visits made to it with
our guide-books. The wondrously delicate mosaics of the architrave were always too dim to
be studied, but now each one has its branch

---

*This obelisk is one of two which Augustus brought with him
from Egypt, and which he intended to place in the CIRCUS
MAXIMUS and the CAMPUS MARTIUS. His death prevented this,
and Claudius had them set up near the tomb of Augustus, where
they remained until thrown down by barbarian invaders. In
1587 Sixtus V. had one of them restored and placed at the foot
of the hill on which Santa Maria Maggiore stands. The inscriptions read thus:

CHRISTI DEI IN ÆTERNUM VIVENTIS CUNABULA LÆTISSIME
COLO QUI MORTUI SEPULCRO AUGUSTI TRISTIS SERVIEBAM—
" I who served with sadness the sepulchre of the dead Augus-
tus. honor gladly the Crib of Christ. the ever-living God."

" QUEM AUGUSTUS DE VIRGINE NASCITURUM VIVENS ADORA-
VIT. SEQ. DEINCEPS DOMINUM DICI VETUIT, ADORO—" Whom
Augustus, when alive, adored as to be born of a Virgin, and
then forbade to be honored with the title of God, Him do I
adore."

CHRISTUS PER INVICTAM CRUCEM POPULO PACEM PRÆBET,
QUI AUGUSTI PACE IN PRAESEPE NASCI VOLUIT—"Christ gives
peace to the world who, by His triumphant Cross, willed to be
born in a manger during the peace of Augustus."

candelabrum filled with wax-lights, and we
remember that each mosaic gives an event drawn
from the Old Testament, quoted by the Fathers
of the Council of Ephesus, 431, as prefiguring
the Divine Maternity of Mary. Through this
avenue of precious mosaics of the years from
432 to 440, bearing witness to the lively faith
in the Incarnation—all ablaze too, as if to honor
it with this testimony of fourteen centuries—we
stand before the triumphal arch to see, on its
ground of gold, those scenes drawn from the
story of the New Testament, which declare His
Incarnation and Nativity, and the wonders attending them; all dating to that magnificent
Council of Ephesus, which declared, with such
joyful acclamation, the Divinity and Humanity
of Jesus, Son of God and Son of Mary—true God
and true Man! It is directly under this Arch of
the Triumph of the Incarnation, on the High
Altar itself, that we shall see exposed, for the
veneration of Christians, the reliquary contain-
ing the precious Crib of the Infant of Bethlehem; and if the early ages of Christianity had
no other proof to give of their love for the Divine
Babe born in a manger, or their utter forgetful-
ness of the humiliation, in the presence of the
joy, this exposition of the Crib on the eve of
Christmas would suffice. The story is one every
Catholic should know by heart, and the sweetness of this flower of Christian tradition should

linger in every household where a cradle is rocked or a mother sings her lullaby.

We have not forgotten the small wooden cradle, with its quaint wooden canopy, in which we were rocked—our brothers and sisters as well; nor those, still more simple, in which the fathers, the mothers, the grandfathers or grandmothers were rocked, and which we had seen stored in family attics and old-fashioned garrets, to be brought down for each generation; only differing, by way of some delicate needlework or feminine decoration, from the cradle of a hundred years before,—when we stood before the grand High Altar of " Saint Mary of the Crib;" nor did we question the exquisitely human tradition which carried us back to the time when no son or heir of a merely princely house made precious the five boards of a wooden Crib, but the Incarnate One, whose will created the light, divided the sea from the land, formed man from the dust of the earth, and then breathed into his nostrils that breath of life which, in man, is "a living soul." There was no question of possibilities or probabilities in all this; it was merely one of the lovely circumstances attending upon the Incarnation and Nativity of Him to whom Saint Thomas of Aquin, in one of his hymns to the Blessed Sacrament, cries out in an ecstacy of love:

"O kind, O loving One !
O Sweet Jesus, Mary's Son !"*

The story is this. The conversion of Constantine proved to be the conversion of his
mother, Saint Helen; and notwithstanding her
advanced years, and the fatigues of such a
journey in those ages, she went to the Holy
Land, not only to kiss the spots which Our Lord
had made sacred by His presence or touch, but
to rescue them from the hands of Pagans, and
give them back to the Christian world as incen-
tives to piety, as well as priceless treasures. It
is to the zeal, as all men know, of this Empress
mother, from whom Constantine must have
inherited many of the qualities which made him
great, that we owe the relic of the True Cross;
and at the same time she discovered the clue to
the poor little Crib in which Our Lord was laid
as an Infant. We know how carefully the
Hebrew people cherished, guarded everything
in the least connected with their faith. Nor
did they lose this habit of veneration on entering the Christian Church. With a delicacy and
fidelity to which we owe the most precious relics
in Christendom, they preserved the memory of
everything connected with the Incarnation,
Life, Passion, Death, Resurrection and Ascen-
sion of Jesus of Nazareth. They might not

---

*O Clemens; O Pie:
O Dulcis Jesu, Fili Mariae !

possess, hold in hand, but they never lost sight of these relics; and when Saint Helen went to Jerusalem, evidence, not to be disputed, attested the verity of these relics. With the joy of a true woman, as well as of a true Christian, she kissed the poor little boards, even then brown with age; absolutely worthless save to the believing soul. But this was not all. With the generosity of an empress, she covered the five boards with plates of silver, and placed them in the Grotto of the Nativity, which she had lined with slabs of marble. All this was about the year 325. From this time the Crib was never lost sight of. So far from this, it drew pilgrims from every part of the world to its side.

In 642 the Orient, and the Sacred places themselves, were over-run by Mohammedans, and all the moveable relics were sent to places of safety; among others, the Crib was sent to Rome, to the church of Santa Maria Maggiore, and deposited in the Chapel of the Crucifix. To this chapel, also, were brought the relics of Saint Jerome, the hermit of Bethlehem, the translator of the Holy Scriptures, and one of the four Latin Doctors; as if his place were still by the Crib of his Infant Lord.

But the silver plates given by Saint Helen are not its only covering. The Crib, with its imperial plates undisturbed, was deposited in a

magnificent reliquary given by Donna Maria
Emmanuel, Duchess of Hermosa. It repre-
sents our Lord as an Infant lying in a Crib,
silver gilt, and enriched with *bas-relievi*, chis-
eled in the same metal; while still earlier, in
1606, Margaret of Austria had shown her devotion to the Incarnation by providing a precious
covering for the Crib of the Divine Infant. The
precise time for removing the relic from its
usual repository in the Chapel of the Crucifix is
before the first Mass called of Midnight, when
it is placed on a temporary altar in the Chapel
of the Crib, as it is named, or sometimes the
Sistine Chapel, as the body of Sixtus V. reposes
here in a beautiful tomb, and under the dome
which he built. Here we see the statue of
Saint John Cajetan holding the Divine Infant
in his arms, as he is said to have done in a
vision. At the end of the Midnight Mass, a
Cardinal Bishop and attendants bring the Crib,
in procession, under a costly case of crystal
given by Philip IV., of Spain, to the High Altar,
where it can be seen and venerated by all the
faithful, and at this altar, before this relic of
the Nativity, is said the Mass of the Aurora.

To speak of the High Altar of Santa Maria
Maggiore on Christmas night, is to recall the
veneration of Christians for the mystery of the
Nativity from the first age of Christianity to
the present. To speak of "The Nativity in

Art," without alluding to this High Altar and its surroundings, is to forget not only the traditions of the Christian religion, but the story of its art.

The Altar itself is an antique sarcophagus of porphyry, on which rests the table of black and white marble, supported by four angels in gilded bronze; and this sarcophagus incloses the relics of Patrician John and his wife, who built the original *Sancta Maria ad Nives.* The canopy, of bronze gilt, is supported by four columns of porphyry, around which are entwined branches of palm in bronze, and the whole is of such magnificence as to fill the eye, in the midst of all the mosaics of architrave and apse. Above this High Altar is that Arch of Triumph of the fifth century, its mosaics set on a ground of gold, and a description of which cannot be too familiar to those who desire to be theologically devout, timing and shaping their devotions according to the spirit of the Christian dogmas, rather than by any private fancy or attraction.

In the middle of the arch is seen an Altar, on which is a book with seven seals. Above this rises a small black cross, veiled, to symbolize the Humanity; and, above this still, a cross, large and studded with gems, standing upon a throne, by which is symbolized the Divinity of Our Lord. All this is given on a medallion,

which is upheld by the two great Apostles, SS.
Peter and Paul, and accompanied by the
winged symbols of the Four Evangelists. On
the same line with the medallion, beginning at
the extreme left for the spectator, is the Annunciation : the Virgin of Nazareth sitting, with
two attendant angels while another seems to
deliver his message. At the same time, in the
air above her, is seen the Dove of the Holy
Spirit, and an angel winging his flight towards
her; two actions in one picture. On the other
side of the medallion, on the same line, is the
Purification, or the Presentation; and never
has it been given in art with more dignity. The
procession of saintly figures, the action of
Simeon and Anne, and even the device to bring
in the two doves which were to ransom the
Divine Infant under the Old Law, are worthy to
be studied, and was studied, we may be certain,
by those who have most successfully represented
it; while it must have entered, necessarily, into
the traditions of art which found their way to
Umbria, and under which Raphael worked when
he painted from his own youthful ideas of this
scene.

On the second zone, below the first—directly,
too, below the Annunciation—is the Adoration
of the Magi, in which Our Lord is represented,
not on His Mother's lap, but sitting erect upon
His throne: the Infant of days, and yet the

Eternal and Omnipotent One. At His side, in the place of honor, stands Mary, majestic even among the angels who attend upon Him behind His throne, while the three kings present their gifts. Opposite this, on the same zone, is the Finding of the Child Jesus in the Temple by Mary and Joseph; and below these two, the Reception of the Wise Men by Herod, and the Massacre of the Innocents. All these were executed by the order of Pope Sixtus III., between the years 432 and 440. But their value is increased by three centuries, when we remember that, although executed at the order of Sixtus, this Pontiff was but carrying out the design of his predecessor, Pope Celestine, who died soon after the Council of Ephesus, and, at his own request, was deposited in the Catacomb of Santa Priscilla, on the Salarian Way, in which these same subjects had been treated before the year 100. Thus our Arch of Triumph in Santa Maria Maggiore, standing above the High Altar on which is exposed the Crib of Bethlehem on this Christmas morning—between the Midnight and the Aurora Mass—is the link which unites the belief of Christians to-day in the Incarnation and the honor paid to the Nativity of Our Lord, and the belief in that same Incarnation, and the honor paid to that same Nativity in the first century of the Christian era. To say that here are no representations before the fifth century, and to argue therefrom that the Nativity was overshadowed by any mystery whatsoever, is to be ignorant of the art of the Catacombs in the year 100; or knowing this, to withhold it.

Is it not time for lay Catholics to study the records of Christianity in her sublime monuments, even when those monuments lie within the shadow of a Catacomb? Can they not afford to leave the pleasant sunshine awhile, in order to set their eyes upon those traces which Christianity has left of its dawn, and the very freshness of its "Hour of Prime." on the walls of a cemetery where were deposited the ashes of a Saint Priscilla, a Saint Pudens, and a Claudia, and where a Pope of the fifth century asked to be laid, among the testimonials so touching, and at the same time so beautiful, of the delight of the Christians of the first century in the Nativity of Our Lord, and all its charming circumstances? Nor can we forget, if we know anything of the signs of the times, that those Catacombs were opened, not for the gratification of our curiosity but as giving us a grand vantage ground on which to make our stand on the questions of the antiquity of our present symbolism, our present ritual, as well as our present form of Christian Art.

Behold on this Christmas morning in Rome, in *Sancte Maria ad Praesepe,* how the Church puts forth her dogmas to the eyes of her children, as well as to their understandings and their hearts!

The glorious colors of her pavement of *Opus Alexandrinum*, the avenue of mighty columns, as through "a forest primeval;" the stories of the Old Testament, told in precious mosaics along her architrave; the stories of the New Testament, in mosaics still more precious, on her Arch of Triumph; and all centering in one point of light where the Adorable Sacrifice of the Redemption is offered on the very Altar where rests the Crib of the Infant who was true God and true Man! "Verily, verily," we seem to hear the voice of this same Jesus saying to us, "the words of the prophets have been fulfilled in your time!"

Do we wonder that the Roman Christmas is no merry-making, no household festivity, no idyl of poesy, no ballad of minstrels, no song-book or folk-lore, but the opening Canto of an Epic as grand as the Incarnation, the Redemption, the Resurrection, in the ages of the Eternity that is past, the Eternity that is present, and the Eternity that is to come?

Let us lift our eyes and behold! Let us lift up our hearts and adore! Let us lift up our voices and praise! Still more: let us yield ourselves up to the mighty genius of Christianity, and allow ourselves to be borne upward and onward by the tides of faith, of hope, of love, coursing through her heart. Let us catch the inspiration of her hymn of praise, and join our voices with hers who is to-day, above all other days, Saint Mary at the Crib!

THE EPIPHANY.

III.

Between the Octave of Christmas and the second day of February comes a feast of such joy and exultation and such grandeur of cir- cumstance, that it has been called the "Gentiles' Christmas." The Epiphany—or manifestation of Our Lord—comes on the sixth day of January, that "Twelfth Night" which is a name associ- ated with everything joyous. This feast takes for its symbol the star which went before the wise men until it stood over the stable "where the young Child was," according to Saint Mat- thew. In her office for this day, the Church brings forward the magnificent prophecy from the sixtieth chapter of Isaiah: "Arise, be en- lightened, O Jerusalem, for thy light is come;" and ends only with that beautiful prediction which was to be fulfilled so literally: "The multitude of camels shall cover thee, the dromedaries of Madian and Epha: all they from Saba shall come, bringing gold and frankincense, and showing forth praise to the Lord;" and for the Gospel, the second chapter of Saint Matthew, giving a full account of the visit of the wise men or the "Three Kings," as they are popularly represented. At the sentence: "They found the Child with Mary His Mother, and falling down they adored Him," all kneel, uniting their adorations with that of the Three Kings. The offertory is from the sixty-fourth Psalm: "The kings of Tharsis and of the islands shall offer presents; the kings of the Arabians and of Saba shall bring gifts; and all kings of the earth shall adore Him; all nations shall serve Him;" and, in the secret, we are told the signification of these offerings. In the antiphons and responsories is gathered all the beauty of prophecy and of Gospel, and the Homily of Saint Leo the Great is like another choral hymn in honor of the Feast of the Manifestation of Jesus Christ to the world. The traditions run that the two other manifestations of Our Lord, viz.: that at His baptism and the first miracle, are commemorated on this day; and one of the Breviary hymns makes mention of all three. The other hymn is familiar to every one:

"Bethlehem! of noblest cities."

But the artists hold fast to the one tradition
of the Three Kings, and the magnificence of the
circumstances has not been overlooked by them.
The coming of the Three Kings often makes the
middle distance, as with Perugino, Raphael and
Lo Spagno, of the Nativity, but is also treated
with untold magnificence by itself. Don Lorenzo
Monaco, a Camaldolese monk, has painted this
subject with so interior a spirit that we know
not how any one can see the aged king on his
knees, and peering with such rapturous adoration into the eyes of the Divine Infant, as if
there he saw Heaven and the beatific vision,
without recognizing, acknowledging the Incarnation. Lionardo da Vinci lays the scene in a
beautiful meadow: the blessed virgin with the
Infant on her knees, under the blue skies; and
troops of attendants follow the Three Kings.
The gorgeousness of this array is made inde-
scribably beautiful by the spirit of gladness
which pervades the whole, and we feel, instinctively, how amiable were all the manifestations
of Our Lord to his creatures. But another
picture gives us the loveliness of the manifestation and the grandeur of the circumstances with
more of the mystery; and this is by Gentile da
Fabriano, in the *Belle Arti* of Florence. The
hall in which this hangs may well be called the
vestibule of Paradise, so transcendently do its

subjects treat of heavenly things. At the side
of this Adoration of the Kings, by Fabriano,
hangs Perugino's Assumption of the Blessed
Virgin contemplated by "the four ambrosial
saints," as they are called, because their very
aspect breathes of the ambrosial air of Paradise;
while at the end of this gallery is Fra Angelico's
Last Judgment, of which the side representing
the good who have received a favorable sentence
and are met by their guardian angels to be con-
ducted to Heaven, is, perhaps, the most blissful
picture in the world. It is among such surroundings that we see, to-day, the Adoration or
Epiphany picture by Fabriano. Here we have
the Virgin Mother and the Infant, and Saint
Joseph at the door of the Cave. Within we see
the manger, the ox and the ass. Before this
humble group come the Three Kings, the most
ancient on both knees, his crown at his side,
while he kisses the foot of the Babe, who touches
with His little hand the head of the old man as
if to bless him. The action of the two other
kings is full of majesty and devotion, and the
attendant of one is loosing the latchet of his
sandal as if he were to make his adoration with
bared feet. In the distance is seen a train
wending toward Jerusalem to give the first part
of the story, while another train issuing from its
gates swells the cortége of the Three Kings. On
he predella are seen the Nativity and the Flight

into Egypt. The whole is one *pæon* of praise and adoration. But we must not omit the grand picture of the Adoration at Cologne by Stephen Lothener, of Constance—one of the glories of the grand Cathedral. We must remember that the relics of the Three Kings are venerated at Cologne, and this will explain the picture, which is not a literal representation of the event, but a glorified one. Here the Virgin Mother, crowned, her blue mantle lined with ermine, sits enthroned, her Child on her knees, her hand under His foot as a token of obedience, of fealty. On either side are the Three Kings and their attendants. The picture is painted on five panels. The Adoration occupies the central one. On the side panels are seen the two great protectors of the city of Cologne : Saint Gereon in armor and surcoat with his men at arms ; on the left, Saint Ursula with her spouse the British prince, Conan, the Bishops and attendants. On the extreme wings is represented the Annunciation. But even with these magnificent representations in mind, we turn with a respect and a tenderness of spirit akin to veneration, to the mosaic of the Adoration on the triumphal arch of the fifth century in Saint Mary Major ; and still more to a painting of the first or at most second century on the walls of the catacombs of SS. Nereo, Achilleo and Domitilla, where the same Virgin Mother is represented seated, her

Divine Child on her knees and the Magi hasten-
ing towards her with their gifts. Not even the
ravages of so many centuries can take from this
work of the primitive Church the charm which
belongs to this lovely subject of Christian art.

Some of the most interesting circumstances
attending the Feast of the Epiphany in Rome
are connected with the College of the Propa-
ganda. There we see all nations represented as
adorers of the Infant Saviour, and hear all languages used in His praise. The altar-piece in
their chapel is an Adoration, the traditional star
assuming supernatural splendor as it stands
over the humble birthplace of the King of
kings.

A stranger in Rome is sure to be surprised at
seeing, on the Eve of the Epiphany, the erection
of numberless booths on the Piazza Navona, on
one side of which stands the beautiful Church of
Saint Agnes; still more surprised to hear that
the Epiphany, not Christmas, is the gift-day in
Rome. All at once, like so many other customs
at this fountain-head of Christian traditions,
the significance and the fitness of this dawn
upon the mind. The shepherds came to Bethlehem in haste, from watching their flocks by
night on the hillsides; and what gifts had they
to bring? The Magi came from afar, prepared,
forewarned that they were to present themselves
before a King who could claim their fealty.

Their gifts were, therefore, timely and even expected. We Americans, so lavish in our generosities, may well imitate the Three Kings in our gifts, not only to our own families and friends, but to those who, having given themselves to God, may well claim our aid in their works of piety and of mercy. With all our generosity we may yet learn something of the duties of Christians from the Three Kings, who, first adoring, opened their treasures and gave their gold, their precious myrrh and sweet frankincense, to the Babe of Bethlehem.

The pomp and glory of the Epiphany have passed before us like a vision. With what tranquility the days wear on, and just before the forty days are over the Cave is once more desolate! The Bethlehemites—have they been altogether blind? Do they now miss some mysterious grace in the air, some unwonted security of their small city? The Holy Family depart as noiselessly as they came, and, instead of a malediction on those who refused them shelter, they have left a blessing, how great, Bethlehem never knew, not even when her infants were torn from her bosom. And now we stand with Jesus, Mary and Joseph in the Temple, with Simeon and with Anne. We see Simeon take the child in his arms, and we hear his *Nunc dimittis*. We see "the old man carry the Child," but we know that "the Child governs the old man." It is the placid ending of forty wonderful days, by the purification of one who was born without sin, and the presentation in the Temple of two Turtle-doves as the price of redemption for Him whose single drop of blood could redeem the world! How joyously the Church takes up the theme! How sweetly she rings her changes on its beautiful traditions. How she weaves her tapestries from the few golden threads of the Gospel narrative! How she lights her thousands and thousands of tapers in honor of Him who is already "a light to the revelation of the Gentiles!" How she leads her processions with Simeon's canticle on their lips, as they defile in shining columns through the naves of her Old World cathedrals, basilicas, and her churches throughout the world, or wherever her traditions are known, are kept, are loved by the people,—loved so well that they can lose one hour from their traffic, their households, to join with Jesus, Mary and Joseph, with Simeon and with Anne, in the *Nunc dimittis,* with its refrain, "A light to the revelation of the Gentiles, and the glory of Thy people Israel!" Time to ponder a moment on that first of Mary's sorrows, the prophecy of Simeon: "And thine own soul a sword shall pierce!" Beautiful Virgin Mother, kneeling in ecstasy over thy new-born Babe in a manger, to hear, in the midst of the Temple, the prophecy

of thy dolors ! Let us not only join the glad procession of the morning, but let us wait upon
this Virgin in the first hours of her first sorrow,
and at evening-song join not only in her
Magnificat, but in the

"AVE MARIS STELLA"

which the Church entones every evening in her
honor. And if Raphael's tender picture of the
Purification and the Presentation is at our
hand, let us take this spring-flower of the second of February, the spring-flower, too, of his
lovely and pious genius, and set it before our
eyes as the loveliest tribute ever paid to her on
the double Feast of the Presentation and Purification.

IV.

Wonderful! Counselor! God the Almighty! Father of the world to come! Prince of Peace! Child that is born for us! Son that is given to us! Star that has risen out of Jacob! Without beginning and without end, and yet a Child of days! How shall we represent this mystery? How shall we declare it unto the generations? To the unlearned as to the wise, to the little ones as to those who have grown old in understanding?

This has been the question put before the Christian artist for these eighteen centuries—the representation of the union of God with man, the Infinite with the finite, the Creator with the creature, the Eternal with perishing mortality—in a word, the Incarnation. Not for one moment

58

can these conditions be overlooked in the representation of Our Lord, whether as the infant in the manger, the Child Jesus in the temple, or the Redeemer on His Cross. From first to last, the Incarnation is to be the dominant thought of the artist, if he is to meet the need of Christendom or to fulfill its ideal. Skill there may be, beauty of forms, loveliness of types; but this one essential ideal lacking, all is lacking. Skill there may not be, forms, types may be crude; but this one essential ideal pervading, informing these imperfect types, and the task has been accomplished. It is upon the Incarnation, as a fact, that the hold of the Christian artist must be taken, if he is to be, not the mere decorator submitting himself to the fashion of his period, but the great instructor of his own and of succeeding generations, the standard-bearer of the God-man!

To begin with the first Christian artist and the first Madonna, we must take Saint Luke the Evangelist; Saint Luke, the "fellow-laborer" of Saint Paul, when the apostle lived with his jailor on the corner of the Via in Lata, Rome, as he mentions in his Epistle to Philemon.

There is a subject of Christian art in connection with Saint Luke which would take us back to the three years' ministry of Our Lord; but this is too wide a field to explore with our present design in mind, and we begin, therefore, with Sain

Luke, as the painter of Madonnas; and go to the prison of Saint Paul, on the Corso and Via in Lata, as the spot where hung for centuries one of the Madonnas painted by Saint Luke, no doubt at the instance of Saint Paul himself. Seven of these Madonnas, according to tradition, were painted by the Evangelist, and one of these is the Madonna which was carried in procession by Saint Gregory the Great during the visitation of Rome by the plague, between the death of Pelagius II., who fell a victim to the pestilence, and the accession of Gregory himself, in 590, to the pontifical throne. The marvelous circumstances attending this procession are thus given by the writers of that day. For the first time, monks and nuns were called from their cells to join in the procession, as well as citizens of all ranks, women, children, even babes carried in the arms of their mothers; all in penitential garb and with bare feet, from the pope to the child; and while they chanted penitential psalms, hymns, litanies, they carried aloft, as a banner, the Madonna of Saint Luke, taken, each time the procession was made, from Santa Maria Maggiore, and returned to it at its close. It was while making the procession on the last, or, as we may presume, the third day, that the eyes of Gregory were opened to see, on the summit of Hadrian's tomb beside the Tiber, which is only a short distance from Saint Peter's on the Vatican, an archangel standing, sheathing his sword as if returning from the combat; and the plague had ceased! From that day to this the tradition concerning this picture has been held as valid, without a break in the testimony of its existence or the place where it has been honored; so that the naming of Saint Luke as the first painter of Madonnas, is no myth but one of those established facts taken note of in every history of art at the present time. Those who visit the Borghese Chapel in Santa Maria Maggiore, still look up to see, above the exquisite altar of *lapis lazuli*, this Madonna by Saint Luke; the precious *lapis lazuli* keeping the hue of the Virgin Mother's mantle above.

But while Saint Luke was in Rome with Saint Peter and Saint Paul, one of the mothers of the Infant Church was living in the house of her son on the Vicus Patricius, or Way of the Patricians. This son was no other than Pudens the Senator, who sent greetings by Saint Paul to Saint Timothy, and the mother was that Priscilla, who was one of the first fruits in Rome of the preaching of Saint Peter. She did not live to be shocked by the double martyrdom of the Church, in the persons of Saint Peter and Saint Paul, on one day. With the absolution of Saint Peter, and under his apostolic benediction, she fell asleep in the Lord, and was carried to the cemetery of her family on the Salarian

Way. Around her, in the course of the generations, were gathered her son, Pudens, and his wife Claudia, their son and his son's sons and daughters, Novatius and Timotheus and Pudentiana and Praxedes. But long before all this had come to pass, Pudens and his wife Claudia carried out the Roman idea of a sepulchre for their mother, Priscilla; and not only the Roman, but the Christian idea. What the Roman idea was it is easy to know from unnumbered pictures of the interiors of their tombs; and the idea of the Christians of that day was to use the same beautiful masonry, the same beautiful arts of design, to express a Christian burial and a Christian hope of the Resurrection. In this instance, the opulence of a senatorial family allowed to Pudens and his wife, and those who were their immediate successors in the pious work, the privilege of expressing Christian ideas in the most perfect manner. We can also understand how a certain filial sentiment suggested a series of pictures which should underlie all other decorations as embodying that essential element of Christian belief—the Incarnation. Around this true "Mother in Israel," who had brooded under her wings the callow converts to the new faith, would naturally cluster those scenes in the Maternity of Mary and the Childhood of Our Lord, which had been described to them, we must believe, not only by the pen of Saint Luke in his Gospel, but by the "word of mouth" of this same Luke, who received them from the Virgin Mother herself, and by this oral narrative had fixed them in their minds as living realities, gracious and most lovely expressions of all that most charms us in the story of the Incarnation. Never, even in the thirteenth, fourteenth or fifteenth centuries, did the apse of any cathedral put forth more blossoms in honor of the Maternity of Mary, than did this subterranean resting-place of the Christian mother of the Christian Pudens during the very lifetime of the Apostles. It is one of the proofs of the fidelity of artists to the traditions of Faith that, although this cemetery or catacomb was closed at an early date, the same subjects, in the same order, with the same dominant ideas, continued to be in use for the decoration of the sanctuary.

First in this order is the Annunciation. In the centre of the ceiling, with the beautiful repose of manner which belonged to the best statues of the best Roman period, sits the young Virgin of the House of David. The robe, with its classic folds, is gathered simply under the virginal cincture; on her head is the veil which, as in Saint Luke's Madonnas, droops modestly on the forehead; one hand still rests on the arm of her chair, the other is raised slightly, as if with surprise at the message of the angel. Before her stands the Archangel Gabriel, one hand on the full drapery which envelopes him, the other extended towards Mary, so as to express all the earnestness of his celestial announcement, and the countenances of both full of a sweetness never to be exceeded. This group is divided from the area of the ceiling by a circle of gem-like decorations somewhat after the manner of the Cosmati mosaics, so much in use many centuries later. From this highly decorative circle are suspended the classic garlands still used in architecture; from their points of attachment to the gemmed circle fall pendants, painted to resemble gemmed crosses; while in the four corners of this square ceiling, each cut off by the gemmed segment of a circle, is a dove on the wing; not, we may believe, merely as the dove so familiar to Rome, or even the dove used to represent Christian souls in the early Christian art, but as the Dove of the Holy Spirit. One can see at a glance that this is no rude style of decoration, but that it agrees, perfectly, with the classic taste shown in the central group.*

Still more remarkably, however, is the veritable Madonna next in order, representing the Virgin Mother with her Divine Child in her arm's, the Child turning from His Mother's

---

*To this day these classic garlands, filled in with the choicest flowers, are suspended around the CONFESSIONS of the great martyrs in Rome on their feast-days, especially around that of Saint Peter in the Vatican.

breast toward the spectator with all the grace
of one of Raphael's most charming infants.
Beside them stands the Prophet Isaias, pointing
to the star over the head of the Mother and
Child, as if to draw attention to that unwilling
prophecy of Balaam,

"A STAR SHALL ARISE OUT OF JACOB."*

The identity of Isaias is proved by other representations of the same subject in other catacombs, in which *a saw*, the symbol of Isaias, or
the instrument of his martyrdom, is given.
De Rossi does not hesitate to say that this Madonna is the most ancient which has been discovered in the catacombs. He invites us to
compare the design, the modeling, the general
style of this painting, with the decoration of
the pagan tombs discovered upon the Latin
Way in 1858, and attributed by all antiquaries
to the time of the Antonines. Vivet, in the
"Journal des Savants," 1866, p. 96, speaks thus
of the Madonna of Saint Priscilla: " There is
such suppleness, such suavity in the modeling, that, without offense to Correggio, we
may say that it would do him honor." This
picture was painted in the most ancient part of
the catacomb of Saint Priscilla, close to the
famous Greek chapel, the masonry of which
proves its antiquity, while its inscriptions

---

* Numbers xxiv., 17.

prove Greek to have been the first prevailing
language of the Church. In another part of
this cemetery, but belonging to a later time,
probably soon after the death of Saint Pudentiana, is painted on one side of the arched space
of the principal tomb a picture of Saint Pudentiana, the great grand-daughter of Saint Priscilla,
receiving the veil of the consecrated Virgin from
the hands of Pope Pius I., A. D. 142-57, accompanied by Pastor who wrote the lives of
the two holy sisters, Pudentiana and Praxedes.
The middle of the arch is filled by the majestic
figure of a woman very richly attired as a
Roman matron, standing with her arms extended in prayer; and under this type of an
Orante or praying woman, we can easily believe
to be represented Saint Priscilla herself. On
the other side of this arch is a Madonna, not
veiled, but seated on a throne-chair, holding
the Divine Infant to her breast while regarding
attentively the group on the other side of the
arch. This picture is believed to have been
painted under the eyes and by the direction of
Saint Praxedes, who laid her sister, Saint
Pudentiana, in her tomb in the cemetery of
Saint Priscilla.

In proof of the frequency of these representations of the childhood of Our Lord, in which His
mother takes the part of a necessary and import-
ant personage, we shall not confine ourselves to

the cemetery of Saint Priscilla. We find in the beautiful cemetery of Saint Domitilla a picture to be referred to nearly the same date, and similar to the Madonna we have described, but without the veil, and instead of a star a city is represented in the background, doubtless Bethlehem, which was given in so many of the mosaics of later centuries. On the walls of this same cemetery of Saint Domitilla, is also to be found an unmistakeable visit of the Magi to the Infant Jesus on the lap of His mother; dating also, unquestionably, to that part of the second century which is close to the apostolic time, i.e., during the lifetime of those who were the immediate disciples of the Apostles and their personal successors. From the arched form of the space on which it is seen, it may have adorned an *arcosolium,* or the principal tomb of a chamber. The Virgin Mother is seated on a throne-chair, the Infant standing on her lap, while two figures, advancing swiftly toward her, are eagerly presenting their gifts. This subject is treated, still again, in the same catacomb, and in this last picture the three traditional Magi appear. In neither representation is the subject to be misunderstood, while in both there is a dramatic action which has not been kept, always, in succeeding times.

Examples of these subjects, and approximating to the same dates, can be quoted from nearly all the catacombs. In the catacomb of Saint Agnes is a Madonna for an altar piece, representing her with all the dignity of a queen, while her Son, past the age of infancy, stands before her in very much the same way as he is seen to stand on the medals of Our Lady of the Sacred Heart; so much so, that one might take the medal for a reproduction of it. This picture is evidently of the time of Constantine, as we see the monogram of the *labarum* at each side.

But there is still another voucher for these pictures, an approbation such as only a successor of Saint Peter can give. The tourist who lingers before the Arch of Triumph in Saint Mary Major, in Rome, has only to look into his guide-book to know that its mosaics date back to the year 431, and to get a tolerably correct list of its subjects. It is, however, to the work of Chanoin de Bleser that he should turn if he wishes to understand them. There is considerable difficulty in studying out these ancient mosaics on a gold ground, especially at such a height. But very accurate drawings have been made from the arch, and these drawings have been photographed so as to assist the traveler in the study of the mosaics from the arch itself.* Their value, archælogically, is

---

*The use of a small hand-mirror greatly facilitates such studies. There are few tourists who have not nearly disjointed their necks by looking at the ceiling of the Sistine chapel, where a hand mirror would have enabled them to see the whole without extraordinary fatigue.

not to be exaggerated, especially if we cons der
why and by whom they were set up before "the
people of God." The well known Council of
Ephesus, convened to establish the dogma of
the Divine Maternity of Mary, was attended
not by Celestine I. in person, but through his
representative, Sixtus the Roman. It was to
commemorate this Council and to honor its
decision, that Celestine planned the Arch of
Triumph for Saint Mary Major. He died soon
after the close of the Council but his successor,
Sixtus the Roman, under the title of Sixtus III.,
fully carried out the intentions of his venerated
predecessor. Moreover, he carried out still
another wish of Celestine I., viz: to have a
picture commemorating the Council which established the Divine Maternity of Mary, placed
in the very catacomb where so many pictures
had been painted in honor of this dogma, that
of Saint Priscilla; as if here were to be found
the pictorial proofs of the belief of Christians
during the first age of Christianity. It was the
catacomb of Saint Priscilla which Celestine
chose for his last resting place, and where he
was actually laid. Of course, both Celestine
and Sixtus III. regarded with veneration the
types delineated in this sacred retreat of the
early Christians, and it must have been with
delight that they found an opportunity to place
them publicly before the eyes of all the faithful.

In the middle of the arch, at the very top, is a medallion supported by the apostles, SS. Peter and Paul, and on the same line as the top of the medallion and the heads of the apostles are the symbols of the four Evangelists. Within the medallion is a small altar, upon which lies the book with Seven Seals, spoken of by Saint John in his Revelation. Above this is a small, dark cross, while, back of the altar and above it, rises a throne resplendent with jewels, and from this throne springs a large and beautiful cross set with gems. These crosses typify the humility and the glory of Our Lord in His Incarnation. On each side of the throne, so as to form the arms is a medallion, in which is a bust representation of the Blessed Virgin. In one of these she is alone; in the other, her Son stands before her, as in the altar-piece of the catacombs of Saint Agnes. Below the medallion and the apostles, is this inscription on a scroll:

"XYSTVS EPISCOPUS PLEBI DEI"

(The Bishop Sixtus to the people of God.)

At the extreme left, as we face the Arch, is depicted the Annunciation. The Virgin Mary is seated, not on a throne, but on a low, decorated stool, attended by two angels. Over her head is the Dove of the Holy Spirit, while the Archangel Gabriel is seen in the air, flying swiftly towards her, and again at her side, delivering his message with great earnestness, and which she hears with the liveliest attention. The group is full of action. Between this and the middle medallion is a representation of the temple, and before it stands Zacharias, with two angels, who announce to him the birth of John the Baptist. On the other side of the medallion, under the arches of the temple, is depicted the Presentation of Our Lord by the Blessed Virgin and Saint Joseph, attended by angels; Simeon receives him into his arms, and Anne the prophetess is seen advancing towards the group with a company of believers. The front of the temple is seen at the right, and doves flutter on the ground before an angel, commemorating the humble offering of two young pigeons, made by these chaste spouses in behalf of the Word made Man. Below this, on the third zone, is represented the coming of the wise men to Jerusalem, inquiring where Christ should be born. On the second zone of the opposite side, directly below the Annunciation, is represented their visit to the new-born Babe, who sits on a richly adorned throne, as if by His own omnipotence. On one side of the throne is the Blessed Virgin, on the other Saint Joseph; over the back of the throne four angelic guards look with admiration upon the Infant, sitting thus erect, while in the air above shines the star which has guided the wise men, who are seen advancing, in regal costume, to offer their gifts to the new-born King. Still below this is seen the massacre of the Innocents, the mothers vainly trying to shield their babes from the soldiers, who are approaching them. On the other side of the arch, Our Lord is represented as a Child with the doctors of the temple, attended by angels, and sought for by Mary and Joseph, with all the vivacity which is seen in later ages. Below these, filling the narrow base of the arch, is seen on one side Jerusalem, on the other Bethlehem, and still below, the mystical sheep, not ranged horizontally one before another, but standing in groups, with a beauty unique in such representations. All these pictures are given on a ground of gold, beautifully finished on the lower edge by a band of mosaic, in the center of which is a medallion, upon it the sign of Constantine's Labarum, and on each side of this the A and Ω ; according to Saint John : "I am Alpha and Omega, the first and the last."

From the year 432, or, at the latest, 440, this arch has attested the belief of Christians in the Divine Maternity of Mary; and from that time there has never failed, in so public a place as the Arch of Triumph in Saint Mary Major, pictorial representations of those scenes in the childhood of Our Lord which have made the fame of so many artists of succeeding times.

It would be an endless work to name over the representations of Mary on the walls of the catacombs, on the glass vessels found in them, on the walls of churches. There is one, however, of the time of Saint Gregory, and in his own palace turned into a monastery, which illustrates the sixth century ideas of Our Lady. The traveler finds it painted on the surface of an irregular niche, looking as if it had been scooped out of the wall, because here the Blessed Virgin ppeared to Gregory, whose one idea seemed to e, to commemorate her visit.

In the subterranean church Saint Clement, Rome, which was closed to mortal eye from before the year 900, until opened under Father Mullooly in the year 1857, are remarkable Madonnas, which show how the Christians of the seventh and eighth centuries regarded these representations. One is an enthroned Madonna, with every regal attribute. On her lap is her Divine Son with His cruciform nimbus, and His mother's hand is under His foot in sign of fealty. It is called the "Madonna of the Niche." Above the niche, in a medallion, is a youthful bust picture of Our Lord, with the cruciform nimbus. The crumbling plaster of the wall still leaves us at the sides of the niche, on one hand the head of Saint Catherine of Alexandria, on a ground studded with stars, and on the other Saint Euphemia, two early

age martyrs. Both wear crowns in which is a
cross, both have the round nimbus, and beside
each is the name running vertically. Below
these heads, and taking up both spaces beside
the niche, is given the sacrifice of Isaac by
Abraham, thus connecting the idea of Redemption with the Babe on the lap of Mary.

On the opposite side of this subterranean
church is a crucifixion, and, we believe, one of
the very earliest representations in fresco of
this scene. Yet it is a crucifixion corresponding
literally to the type of the crucifixion in succeeding centuries, unless in having the four
nails instead of three. We may also remark,
that the horizontal position of the arms is in
perfect accordance with the highest authorities
in this matter. There is a gross dereliction
from the true type in many of the crucifixes in
use at present, which has been stigmatized, by
exact theologians, as a shadow left by the Jan-
senists on the art of our time. In these crucifixes, the arms are often held almost vertically,
as if Our Lord's weight dragged on the nails,
doing violence to the idea of a voluntary sacrifice, and degrading the figure of the Redeemer
by a resemblance to the writhing, struggling
figure of the bad thief! Exactly contrary to all
ᴣhis, is the figure of Our Lord on His Cross in
the subterranean church of San Clemente, giving the ideas of the ninth (or more probably the

seventh and eighth), century Christians. In
this picture, as we have said, the arms are
nearly horizontal, the head is inclined quietly
to one side and raised a little, as if giving forth
that agonized cry: "My God, my God, why hast
Thou forsaken me!"

On the right side of the Cross stands Mary in
veil, mantle and nimbus, stretching both hands
towards her Son in an agony of grief; on the
left side is Saint John, young, beardless, with a
nimbus, one hand raised beseechingly to his
Lord, the other holding a roll, as an Evangelist.
At the side of this picture is represented the
Holy Sepulchre, with an angel by the door, addressing the two holy women as they approach
it. Below this is the descent of Our Lord into
Limbo, where he raises from his recumbent
position the first man, Adam, who lays one hand
on his breast in token of gratitude, while Eve
stretches forth both hands to her Lord in supplication. Still below this is seen the upper
part of the marriage in Cana of Galilee, and we
may say that in no picture, ancient or modern,
has the type of Our Lord been more beautifully
preserved. The cruciform nimbus crowns the
benign head, and the eyes are inclined down-
ward with an expression like that which Lionardo gave to Our Lord in His Last Supper.
Close beside Our Lord stands Our Lady, veiled,
with her nimbus, holding up her hands in won-

der and admiration; at her side is Saint John, the spaces being filled with heads and figures on an architectural background. The falling plaster has deprived us of the lower part of this beautiful picture.

But perhaps the Madonna, which is the most of a surprise in this subterranean church, closed since the ninth century, is an Assumption! An Assumption, too, a good deal after Titian's own heart; full of joy, of exultation, of gesture, and even of awe! In the middle of the foreground stands an empty tomb; above this appears the Blessed Virgin ascending in the air, her arms extended, and her face turned towards her Divine Son, who is seen above her in an oval glory up-borne by angels, the background sown with stars. Our Lord is sitting on a rainbow in one hand a book, the other extended as if to welcome His mother. Below, on the same line as the empty tomb, are the Apostles; some following the receding figure of the Blessed Virgin with their eyes, others throwing her a last farewell with uplifted hands, others hiding their eyes as if they could not see her taken away from them, even to go to Heaven! At the extreme left side of the group is a figure looking out from the picture, named Saint Vitus, in letters which stand vertically below each other. His head is shaven like that of a monk, and is crowned with a nimbus. In his hand he carries a small cross. On the extreme right is another figure, looking out of the picture also, but with a square nimbus, with a small cross at the top, around his shaven head, showing that this person was still living when the picture was painted. He wears a pallium, marked with black crosses, and carries a book in his hand. On each side of the square nimbus are the letters of an inscription which reads thus: "That this picture may outshine the rest in beauty, behold the priest, Leo, has studied to compose it," with the name, "Leo, Pope of Rome." Father Mullooly says it is not easy to decide whether Leo III. or Leo IV. is intended. If Leo III., the picture must have been painted before 795; if Leo IV., before 847. In either case it is a date sufficiently ancient to cause one to withhold any animadversion on the propriety of painting the Assumption of the Blessed Virgin.

We could go on from this date through the tenth, eleventh, twelfth, thirteenth, fourteenth, fifteenth, sixteenth centuries, quoting Madonnas, and comparing them with the early Madonnas. But this would take us far beyond the limits proper for this article.

We almost promise to do this in the future, however; for never until within the last twenty years could this have been done satisfactorily. The opening of the catacombs in connection with the Arch of Triumph in Saint Mary Major has given an entirely new aspect to the subject of Madonnas. Only a few days ago we took up a history of art—one considered of undoubted authority—in which it was stated that, while Our Lord is often seen standing on the knee of His Mother in early Christian art, He is never seen in her arms; while we have to-day, in the earliest picture of the Madonna as yet found in the catacombs, and that before the year 100, a picture of the Infant Jesus turning from the breast of His Mother as she holds Him in her arms! The ignorance of the past is to be excused; but in a few years such a statement will invalidate any author's testimony.

As we have said, these discoveries of Madonnas in the catacombs, are invaluable archæologically, but this is not all. These discoveries are invaluable as confirmations of Christian faith. How many Catholics have a lingering trust of *so many Madonnas*, as if their number and variety implied some excess of devotion to Our Lady! How many Protestants, also, who have a sincere admiration for this Virgin Mother,

" Our tainted nature's solitary boast."

according to Wordsworth, are still a little afraid of some of the Madonnas; for instance, those representing her Assumption! For both of these classes, more numerous than many are aware, these pictures of the early Madonnas contain both encouragement and instruction. To know that our veneration for the Blessed Virgin is the very same as that cherished for her by Christians in the first century down to those of the ninth, is a confirmation of pious confidence too sweet, too precious, to be overlooked or forgotten. Neither is there any one so fervent that his piety is not quickened by such evidences of the devotion of those far-away ages towards the Incarnate Word and his Virgin Mother.

V.

Madonna! Loveliest word in the loveliest of all languages spoken by human tongue! Madonna! word fragrant as breezes from the spice islands of India, with all that moves the affections of mortal hearts, all that stirs them to devotion! Madonna! The keynote of dogma, the cypher by which we spell out the mystery of the Incarnation. Madonna! The inspiration of the Christian poet, as thou hast been of the masters of Christian song, the Cecilians of the ages; but above all, the inspiration of Christian artists, from the unknown decorators of the catacombs of Santa Priscilla and Santa Domitilla, and the Arch of Triumph in Santa Maria Maggiore, to Giunta of Pisa, Guido, Duccio, Simone Memmi, Ansano and Sodoma of Siena, Cimabue and Giotto of Florence, Jacopo Turrita the Franciscan in his mosaics, Nicolo Pisano in marble, Andrea Pisano in bronze, down to the richest efflorescence of Christian art under Ghiberti, Donatello, Lorenzo di Credi, Leonardo da Vinci, Luini, Fra Angelico, Perugino, Gentile da Fabriano, Giovanni Santi, Lucca della Robbia, Michael Angelo, to Raphael himself; as if to prove that art, above poetry, or music, or any outcome of human genius, owes its inspiration to those dogmas of which the Incarnation is the life and the very soul.

Yet, if we must choose, from all this galaxy of radiant names, one which may stand as an exponent of the whole, the swing of whose pendulum describes the entire arc of beauty, of tenderness, of sublimity, we must undoubtedly choose that of Raphael Santi of Urbino. To show how this transcendent gift was sheathed in the giving, let us go back to the home in which Raphael was born, beyond question, " in a happy hour," although on Good Friday, 1483; the home of his father, Giovanni Santi, and his mother, Magia, and still to be seen on the *Strada del Monte* in Urbino.

As one would say, perhaps, differing in nothing from a hundred homes in its neighborhood, we no sooner throw the light of a strong reflector upon this home on the *Strada del Monte*, than we find it a nest to which God has confided

the genius which is to delight not only Italy, but
the world; not only delight, but make hap-
pier and better; who is to be its joy and con-
solation, and the spur to its devotion; not only
in cathedrals and chapels, not only in palaces,
but in the fairest and humblest home of Christendom. He is to be, this God-bestowed genius—
for God alone confers genius since it is confined
to no rank, no family, can be secured by no
painstaking and by no education—the possession
of entire humanity; it has been given to him to
touch every spring of human feeling, sentiment,
emotion, aspiration; and the nest where he was
born, was nourished, was fledged, was this
Christian home on the *Strada del Monte*. Come
with me to it; knock at the modest door; enter
the spacious but unostentatious apartments.
Still better, meet there the pious, affable poet
and painter, Giovanni Santi; his lovely, gentle,
pious wife, and the angelic boy to whom they
gave, so fitly, the name of Raphael; from his
very birth an angel of beauty, of amiability, of
tender piety. But the atmosphere of this home,
how shall we describe it? An atmosphere of
peace, for it was an atmosphere in which Giovanni Santi could paint Madonnas. An atmosphere of love, of the sweetest domestic happiness, for here it was that Giovanni Santi found
models for his holy families in Magia, the
grandmother Elizabetta, and the angelic babe

Raphael. An atmosphere of devotion, for here it was that visions of celestial adoration came to Giovanni, and he became known over Italy as "a painter of the Madonna." The favorite pastime of the little Raphael was to play with the brushes and colors in his father's studio, and his first recollections went back to some Madonna, on his father's easel, for which he had heard expressed some extraordinary praise. The life led by this family of the *Strada del Monte* was not only a good Christian life, but an ideal Christian life. Saints and angels, their feasts, their patronage, came into the daily routine of this household, which was not content with the crumbs dropped from the Christian table, but sat as guests at the board and partook of its heavenly delights. That charm which invests the dogmas, the practices of a Christian's year, and a Christian's week, and a Christian's day and even hour; which makes the sound of the Angelus bell so dear, the recitation of the Angelus so consoling; which makes the Rosary a veritable string of meditations as beautiful, as poetic, as the roses of Persia; which makes the Vespers and the Benediction, though not of obligation, so sweet that some joy seems to have dropped out of the Sunday or the festival when we have missed them; this charm was felt, and understood, and fully valued by the family of the Santi, on the *Strada del Monte*. There was an ideal element in this household, in every member of it; there was a tenderness of culture, and a gentleness of affection, which made piety something more than an obligation—a most sweet attraction.

Nothing lovelier as a merely human household was ever known on earth than this household on the *Strada del Monte* in Urbino, but this did not save it from sorrow. Our Raphael was only seven years old when his, grandmother, Elizabetta died—and someone has said that no household is perfect without a grandmother—and only four days after, his mother, Magia, was snatched by death from the home which might be called the ideal home of a Christian family. Then it was, that the boy Raphael became his father's constant companion, accompanied him to the cities where he was called to paint, and again stood for his father's Saint John Baptists and Saint Raphaels. But this was only for three years. At eleven years of age Raphael was an orphan. No one can say what was the effect of all this upon the imagination of the wonderful boy to whom God had given what God alone can bestow, not only life, but the genius which vivifies the lives of others. It was to his mother's brother, Simone Ciarla, that Providence kindly confided the noble and delicate nature and the budding genius of Raphael. Of his gifts and his predilection there could be no

question, and he was placed under that master,
Perugino, who had been called by Giovanni
Santi himself, "a divine painter." In the studio of Perugino, all the most sacred traditions
of Umbria were faithfully nourished in the soul
of his pupil, and thus the aroma of those first
tender years on the *Strada del Monte* was never
dissipated. One of the first fruits of this train-
ing of the heart, the imagination, the ascetic as
well as the æsthetic capacity of this favored
soul, was the Espousals. It was the spring
flower of Raphael's genius; not only because of
his youth, for he was not yet twenty-two years
old, but by reason of its virginal tenderness, modesty, reserved grace, and even by the beauty of
its coloring, which has always been described as
that of the first blooms of spring, How can we
pass over the story in which the "Espousals," of
Raphael, as well as of Perugino, had its root?
The ring of the Blessed Virgin, her marriage
ring, brought to Perugia, how it was secured for
that city by the devotion of the great captain,
heroic penitent, chivalrous knight of the Blessed
Virgin, Braccio Baglione, and how, from this,
sprang that lily of Christian art, the Espousals
of Our Lady; all this must be read on the truly
Catholic pages of M. Rio in his work *L'Art
Chretien*, if we would see it in its fullness of
beauty; and the picture itself, in its reproduc-
tions, why has it not a place among marriage

gifts to our lovely Catholic brides, as well as
silver, or laces, or even pearls?

Soon after this our Raphael makes his first
visit to Florence, and how must he not have
charmed the hearts of those Catholic Floren
tines of the sixteenth century, to whose favor
genius was the passport which wealth is to ours?
And Florence? For the first time since his
infancy, literally his seventh year, domestic
life, under its most delightful aspects, sur-
rounded Rapael. The beautiful Florentine
mothers, the beautiful Florentine children, the
charms of affectionate intercourse, how they
recalled the gentle Magia, the ideal Giovanni,
the grandmother Elizabetta, the little sister he
remembered to have seen, early as she died, in
their arms? The households of Florence were
thus lighted up by the far-off radiance of the
dearly cherished memory of the home on the
Strada del Monte. It was during this visit that
he painted for his friend Lorenzo Nasi and his
young bride, the lovely *Madonna Cardellino,*
or the Madonna of the goldfinch. In the midst
of a far-spreading landscape sits this maiden
Mother; in the hand dropped at her side, that
book of prophecies which Mary alone could then
fully understand; botween her knees leans the
Divine Child, as if supported by them, and the
little Saint John brings him a goldfinch, with a
look of such love as only the Child Jesus could

inspire; while the Infant Emmanuel lays His baby hand on the head of the little goldfinch with the majesty of the Creator blessing His creature. See how the human and the Divine are wedded in this Infant of days, and tell, if you can, whence, but from the Incarnation, as the web and woof of Raphael's thought, and fancy, and imagination, came this wonderful revelation to the young man of twenty-two.

While in Florence, with a touch as light as the brush of a humming-bird's wing past the flower, came the *Madonna Gran Duca;* so tenderly serious, so sweetly meditative, the eyes of the mother entranced by the Infant on her arm. A thin tissue of white is drawn across the hair and forehead, and you can see that the mantle rests on the head. The Child on His mother's arm, one hand on her shoulder, the other on the drapery of her bosom, as if He said, "Here is my nourishment," looks out from the picture as the Child whose "name is Wonderful, the Counsellor," fed by a drop of milk from the breast of a Virgin Mother. The pathos, the tranquility, the sublimity of this *Madonna Gran Duca,* whence had it root, if not in that dogma of the Incarnation upon which Raphael had fed from the moment of his birth?

The short visit to Florence was over, and there was a return to Perugia; a short sojourn, but full of work and full of patronage. It was the patronage of Atalanta Baglione, a sister of Braccio, which he took with him to Florence on his second visit; an order for that "Entombment" which is one of the treasures of the Palazzo Borghese in Rome. But once in Florence, Madonnas sprang into life as flowers under the skies of April. They are scarcely to be counted, still less described, for the Florentine families did not covet realistic portraits so much for their homes, as we of to-day; they coveted rather that ideal presence, that image of celestial benignity, which goes under the name of Madonna; the sinless Mother and the Divine Child. Who ever heard of a Florentine of the fourteenth, fifteenth and sixteenth centuries, saying there were "too many Madonnas?" Who ever heard of a Florentine, whether prince or *contadino*, asking for "more expression" in the serenely beautiful face of the Mother Immaculate looking down upon him from the altar of his parish church, or of his private chapel? Among the exquisite conceptions of this happy period of Raphael's life, is that "Madonna of the Field," which is similar to the "Madonna of the Goldfinch"; also the *Madonna del Passeggio,* in which Our Lady is walking with her Son through beautiful meadows, where they are met by the little Saint John with his reed cross, who kisses the young Jesus with the most ardent affection, while in the distance is seen Saint Joseph.

These Madonnas, all with a most charming landscape as a background, may be said to find their perfection in *La Bella Giardiniera.* Everything graceful in the others we have mentioned is seen in this, with all the beauty of scenery; but there is a perfection in the Mother's beauty, in the sweetness of her maternity, also in the majesty of the Divine Infant, and in the adoration of Saint John, which surpasses any similar expression in his former pictures, and shows how perseveringly Raphael endeavored to realize his ideal.

There is another picture belonging to this time, now to be found in Munich, called "The Whispering Madonna." The Mother is standing as gracefully as a rose bending backward on its stalk, to support her Child, pressing his face close to her own. There is a sweet smile on her lips, and the Child?——Have you never seen a mother holding her lips to her child's ear and whispering—whispering, oh, how softly and sweetly? And have you not seen the infant's face change, smile, look grave, smile again, all as if it understood every word said in its ear? This is what you see in this "Whispering Madonna." But this is not all. You realize, as perhaps never before, unless in reading some page from Father Faber, the blissful familiarity in which Our Lady lived with her Divine Babe. There was a veneration, oh, how tender, for the least fold of linen touching His sacred Body; there was an adoration, oh, how absolute, for His Divine Person; at the same time Mary handled, caressed, soothed the charming Humanity of the little Incarnate One with all a mother's fondness, all a mother's caresses. There was no timidity, no reserve. He was, verily, her Son, and she was, verily, His Mother; and never, even between Eve and her Innocent children, was there ever such an unrestrained affection as between the Child Jesus and the Virgin Mother whose name was Mary. Furthermore, the picture tells us of the understanding by speech and word, by ear and hearing, between this Mother and this Son. She whispers into the ear of the Divine Child, and He understands and listens to her; answers her, too, in the language mothers understand from their infants. Raphael's infant tongue had lisped the Hail Mary like every other child of Catholic Italy, and when he painted his "Whispering Madonna," he painted it as one who believed that the least accent from that mother's lips was heard, was regarded, was answered by the son in her arms. It was an *Ave Maria* which he painted under the form of a Whispering Madonna.

There is a touch of youthful enthusiasm, of ardent expectation, a laying hold of a great hope, in the account given us of the haste with which Raphael responded to a call from Rome; a call,

too, from no less a person than the Sovereign
Pontiff, Julius II; how he left Florence and all
its attractions, fully taking in the wonderful
possibilities before him in the Eternal City.   As
he afterwards writes with his characteristic in-
genuousness to his uncle (whom he always ad-
dresses in his letter, " dear to me as a father ") :
"Is there any place better than Rome?" Raphael understood that the patronage was beyond
that of kings or of governments, and leaving the
blue mantle of an Enthroned Madonna to be
painted in by a friend, he hastens to the Vatican,
to the feet of Julius II., who was succeeded by
Leo X., and under both pontiffs executed works
which draw to the Vatican travelers from the
entire world.   It would be well worth while to
throw as strong a light upon the *Disputa*, the
most wonderful picture ever painted in honor of
the Blessed Sacrament, as we see thrown, by
learned commentators and skilled engravers,
upon the school of Athens.   But at this present
time we are pledged to the Madonnas executed
by Raphael, in his latest Roman manner, as it
is called; in reality, the manner into which
his ideas of Mary, Virgin and Mother, with her
Divine Son in her arms, were sublimated by the
ripening of his genius and his devotion to the
dogma of the Incarnation.

There was never a time when Raphael was not
ready to answer a call for a Madonna; never a

time when the call did not give him a sense of
fresh delight. It was a renewing of the early in-
spirations, of the sweet Umbrian traditions of his
childhood. The coldest of his critics will say,
in a matter-of-fact way: " Raphael was never so
much at home as with his Madonnas." And so
it was, that all through the grand Roman period
of his life, when his genius was ever on the wing,
ever on the ascendant, Madonna after Madonna
flitted in between the great frescoes of the *stanzi*,
the *loggie*, the cartoons for the tapestries, the
ceilings of churches and villas. Moreover, the
designs for the ceilings, certainly if mythologi-
cal, would be given to his pupils to execute ; but
the Madonnas would be painted by his own
hand. Among these precious tributes to the Incarnation, is the Madonnas of the Duke of Alba, a
round picture, most delicately painted. As in
so many others, this group is in the midst of a
lovely landscape. The Mother has been reading,
the volume still in her hand, when the little Saint
John, in his impulsive way, kneels before the Infant slipping from His Mother's lap and presents to Him a cross ! Only his own slender reed
cross ; but the action brings a look of prophetic
sadness to the Mother's face. It is one of the
very few Madonnas painted by Raphael which
would not be called joyous ! In almost every
other, this divine Little One brings to His Mother
that fullness of joy, that happiness known only

to those who possess Him; and over this happiness seldom falls even a shadow of the coming sorrow.

Another, is the "Madonna of the Diadem," or "of the Veil," or, as some call it, "Silence." The Child is sleeping in a charming spot, not far from picturesque ruins, in all the beauty of dewy infantine slumber, one arm over His head. At His feet kneels the beautiful Virgin Mother, one arm around the Saint John kneeling beside her, his plump little hands clasped in the rapture which lights up his whole face as she raises the thin veil thrown over the divine Slumberer. What child could ever see this picture without wishing to kneel with Saint John and adore!

Two pictures, similar but still unlike, with a different key-note of sentiment, are deserved favorites; and yet, very seldom do they find right interpreters: *Madonna della Sedia*, or the Madonna of the Chair; and *Madonna della Tenda*, or the Madonna of the Curtain. Both are seated, both are painted in warm flesh tints and with rich draperies, both hold the Child in the arms, and in both Saint John adores. In the *Madonna della Tenda*, Saint John seems to have spoken, and the Infant turns His head as if to listen to him, and the face of the Virgin shows that she hears also. In the *Madonna della Sedia*, there is an intensity of happiness, a concentration of thought, which is seen in no other

perhaps, until the last one ever painted by
Raphael. The soft meditative eyes of Mother
and Child look out from the picture, as if there
were an eternity in their happiness. The Everlasting, without beginning, of days, reposes on
that throne before which must ever pale the
thrones of ivory, or gold, the lap of His Virgin
Mother, and is encircled by her arms; while in
a mist of negative tints, as contrasted with the
positive ones we have in the two principal figures,
stands Saint John in a veritable trance of adoration. This is one of the treasures of the Tribune
of the Pitti Gallery, Florence.

As a contrast to these passively beautiful
groups, is one of such richness in conception,
of such delicacy in detail, so profound in meditation, so intense in action, so harmonious in
the very flow of its lines, that it wins the heart
at one look. The Virgin Mother is seated on a
grassy bank in the shadow of a court yard.
There is an opening of the arches giving a
glimpse of sky, and Saint Joseph is approaching. On her knee Mary bears her Son, who is
leaning eagerly forward towards the little Saint
John in loving adoration at His feet. Beside
the Blessed Virgin sits Saint Elizabeth, who is
holding up the arm of the Divine Child that He
may bless her son, His precursor, and His prophet; and all this while Mary, not beholding his
face, but enraptured by the sweetness of her

Babe, sits with blissfully joined hands adoring Him whom her soul loves. It is called the "Madonna of Divine Love!"

Now we have the *Madonna da Foligno*, painted for the Church of *Ara Cœli*, beside the Capitol. Enthroned on the clouds of Heaven, an arch of Cherubim and Seraphim above her, sits this Lady and Mother, her finger slipped lightly under the sash, by which she seems to hold the Child, almost ready to spring from her arms to those who are addressing Him from below. One of these is the venerable donor of the picture, presented to the Court of the heavenly Infant by Saint Jerome, his lion at his side. Opposite stands Saint John as the precursor, in his hand the reed cross of the *Agnus Dei*, pointing to Him who is to come, and beside Saint John kneels the Seraph of Assisi, pleading for sinners and for the world. Between these groups stands the "Cherub with the tablet," as he is called, gazing upward. In the far distance is a city which is spanned by the rainbow of peace; for this picture was an *ex voto*, acknowledging a deliverance from some tempest.

What a different group is that of the *Madonna Del Pesce* or fish, but how perfect in conception, how worshipful in all its details! Our Lady is on a throne. We see the sky, a mountain summit, just beyond the sweep of the heavy window drapery. One foot of the Child touches her lap, but she holds Him up lightly on both hands. Beside them stands Saint Jerome in his character of Doctor, reading from a heavy tome, the Scripture he has translated, the lion of Bethlehem and of the desert beside him. He has been reading to his Infant Lord, by whose crib in Bethlehem he had made his famous translation at the order of Pope Damasus, as if asking the approbation of the Child on his labors. But as he reads, a boy approaches; the young Tobias led by the Angel Raphael. The boy, kneeling with the timid reverence of youth, presents a fish to our Lord, and the Archangel supports his charge with all the tender concern of an Angel Guardian. Meanwhile, the Infant, not to slight the great Doctor, Saint Jerome, keeps one hand on the page he was reading when interrupted, as if to mark the place; while the the other is extended, with a majestic benignity, a supreme grace, towards the Archangel and Tobias. In all this there is, absolutely, nothing left to desire.

The Madonna of the Duke of Alba had left much untold; and now the call comes from the monks of *Santa Maria dello Spasimo* at Palermo, Sicily. The very name of the convent suggested that scene where the spasm of an unutterable anguish seizes the heart of the Mother of Sorrows, as she sees her Divine Son falling under His cross. The long arms, so beautiful in their

gesture of supplication, the hands attenuated by
one night of agonized watching but beautiful in
their attenuation, the whole figure giving its cry
of anguish as she tries in vain to assist Him,
tell how the heart of this Mother had contracted
in one spasm of mortal agony. We have Simon
of Cyrene, we have the guards on foot, we have
the mounted soldiers and the centurion in fair
armor, and the caparisoned steeds hold themselves proudly; and yet all this show of world's
pomp and brief authority cannot dwarf the Divine majesty of Him who has been trodden upon
as "a worm and no man," and now, prone upon
the earth which He had come to redeem with all
its millions on millions of human souls. The
eyes of Mary meet the eyes of her Son, and they
understand each other as they did in the dear
days of Bethlehem and Nazareth, when they
whispered sweetly to each other. There is the
sorrow of the God-man, but there is the beauty
of the God-man also; and on the tips of those
slender fingers, clutching, as He falls, the rock
of the roadside, or still holding His cross, the
master has set the seal of a divine beauty even
in suffering. The story of this picture is one to
be remembered. The ship on which it was to
go to Palermo was wrecked; crew, cargo, all
lost. But one day Genoese sailors saw a box
floating on the waves, picked it up, and when
opened, *Lo Spasimo*, the Madonna of Sorrows,

transfixed all hearts. This waif of the sea Genoa claimed, stoutly, against all the entreaties of the Monks of Palermo, until the picture was restored to them by the express command of the Sovereign Pontiff.

But the Monks of San Sisto at Placentia must have a banner, and from Raphael. A banner to float under that clear sky, in that atmosphere next to that of heaven. The imagination of the artist kindled, glowed. His whole soul melted into a flame of devotion. There was a grand summing up of all belief, of all tradition; Umbrian, Roman; a summing up, too, of all personal devotion, the life-long attraction, the never outgrown but ever increasing tenderness of personal love to the Mother and the Son, the Incarnation and the Redemption. No studies were made, no model posed. With the swiftness of light the red chalk struck the outline of the woman of the Apocalypse; but without moon or stars, bearing only as the insignia of her matchless nobility, her ineffable purity, the Son born of a Virgin in her arms, on her bosom; the feet not so much as resting on the clouds over which she moves through the infinitude of space.

This atmosphere, what is it? Myriads of angels make the serene distances from which she has glided in her virginal serenity, and we see them faintly delineated until they melt into the immediate glory that surrounds this pres-

ence of hitherto unconceived majesty. From
the head floats off, with the breezy swelling of a
sail, the veil of the Virgin. The hair is parted
and drawn smoothly from the forehead. The
eyes look out upon the world, upon the universe
itself, with all the clearness of knowledge, all
the modesty of virginity. One arm, so assured
in its motherhood, upholds the Child as upon
a throne; the other hand, under His arm presses
Him to her bosom, and His head is brooded
under her cheek. Resting thus, this superb
Being, uncreated and yet born, the mystery
of eternal ages kindling within the shadows
of His Infant brows, looks out on the worlds
He has created, on the souls he has redeemed;
the self-sustained centre of inconceivable space.
On one side kneels Saint Sixtus, the embodiment
of Pontifical venerableness, of Pontifical inter-
cession. On the other, Saint Barbara, as be-
nignant in her exaltation as when the tower
beside her opened its three windows for the conversion of her father. She listens to the *ora pro
nobis* of her clients, and turns upon them a look
of compassion. Below, as if resting on Heaven's
own parapet, lean two beautiful angels, gazing
in rapture on the Presence above, their rainbow
tinted wings sending into a mystical distance
whatever is beyond them, while the whole comes
before one as if the dark green curtains of some
upper room in Rome had opened, to disclose to

the eyes of the Faithful a vision of celestial, everlasting beatitude !

This was the last Madonna painted by Raphael, as the Transfiguration was his last composition. There was no setting sun to his day of life; rather, like the morning star, his brightness passed into the dawn of an eternal day.

No attempt has been made here to enumerate the Madonnas painted by Raphael. The impulse was to give such as might be considered types of whole families of Madonnas painted by the artists of all Christian ages. There was no attempt with any of them at originality; merely an endeavor to attain to some ideal existing, not only in the soul of the artist, but in the mind of the community, the people, the society in which they lived. Italy, Spain, Portugal, France, Germany, demanded Madonnas. One sentiment pervaded artists and patrons, and the picture of the Aldobrandini Madonna, with its pink, sanctifies a flower beloved by the peasant, the artisan and the prince. In vain shall we analyze their beauties in order to reproduce them. They belong to an ideal generation as well as to an ideal painter; to a generation in which dogma or belief, practice or piety, were invested by that charm so rare in our day; which belongs to Christian æsthetics, and to be acquired not so much by specified studies, as by a sentiment which pervades all studies, directs the choice of acquisition, and, when it has found "the pearl of great price," knows how to "sell all it possesses" and secure it.

The home in which Raphael was born, endowed with the heritage of Christian ideality, may well excite the emulation of the fathers and mothers of to-day. It was not the occupation of an artist, the mere handling of the implements of art, which - made that home so attractive; so powerful, too, as an incentive to perfection. It was rather the sentiments of piety, of veneration which guided its avocations, refined its manners, elevated its tastes; above all, it was the faithful cherishing of the traditions of piety which had come down with the ages, and which made each generation a participator in the heroism, the sanctity of all which had gone before, even to the Apostolic day and generation. It is only in such a society that such works as the Madonnas of Raphael can be produced, or even appreciated. We must come, as they came, loving worshippers to the Crib of the Babe of Bethlehem. We must kneel there with Mary and Joseph, and Saint John Baptist and Elizabeth, if we would enter into our possession, as Christians, of that poetry in art which is an exponent of the highest faith as well as of the highest culture.

Madonna! Sweetest word in the sweetest language spoken by mortal tongue. Madonna!

Word powerful to destroy all heresies as to exalt imaginations. Madonna! Come with Thy Divine Son in Thine arms, and breathe over this land, so barren in its civilization, so unattractive in its enlightenment. Come! Breathe over us until the time of the flowers shall come, and the voice of tradition be heard in our homes; until the young men and the maidens shall take Thee as their Mother and Patroness, and every child shall be a Saint John, to adore the Divine Infant on thy knees, O Virgin Mother of God!

ERRATA.

Page 64, line 24, read *remarkable* for remarkably.
" 64, " 27, " *arms* " arm's.
" 78, " 20, " *distrust* " trust.
" 86, " 24, " *between* " botween.
" 91, " 21, " *School* " school.
" 92, " 10, " *Stanze* " stanzi.

www.ingramcontent.com/pod-product-compliance
Lightning Source LLC
Chambersburg PA
CBHW020808020726
47495CB00008B/2636